WILLING CHAFF

WILLING CHAFF
Copyright © 2026 by JA Huss
Cover design by JA Huss
ISBN: 978-1-957277-57-8
All rights reserved.

ABOUT THE BOOK

48 Hours. No Limits. No Mercy. No Excuses.

ScarletSins

Check here if you agree to be hunted. Yes.

Check here if you agree to be caught. Hell yes.

I told myself the first time was desperation. The second time is just... follow-up. Fact-checking. Character development. Research.

Why am I doing this again?

Story fodder.

That's what I keep telling myself.

The auction starts in three hours and I've already checked the box I swore I wouldn't.

Run.

Watcher

Check here if you've been counting the days. Every single one.

Check here if you let her think this was her idea. Obviously.

She came back. Told herself it was for the writing. Told herself she's gathering material. She has no idea what I'm gathering.

Why am I doing this?

Because watching isn't enough anymore.

The auction starts in three hours and the hunt is already over.

She just hasn't stopped running yet.

This book contains: a man who should be in prison, a woman who should know better, and scenes that will make you google "is this okay?" (It's not. Enjoy.)

VIBE WARNINGS

👁️📹🖤 He's always watching
🔪⚖️💀 Serial Killer with a Code
🛏️😰🪟 Your therapist will have questions
▶️⛓️🖤 Trust issues are justified
👻🔥💀 Sorry not sorry
🏃⛓️💀 She runs. Not fast enough
🐺👁️🔥 Prey/predator dynamics
👆💀🗡️ Touch her and find out
⚫🔒✅ Safe words are used
⛓️💔🖤 Trauma bonding
🔪💀🩸 Murd3r & Tortvr3

CHAPTER 1
CALEB

The world's worst men shake the most hands.

The movie star who violates children.

The CEO who traffics them.

The politician whose foundation supplies both.

The spotlight doesn't expose monsters—it blinds you to them.

Before me are two walls of monitors with two very different scenes.

On the left wall of monitors we have Dimitri Volkov. Friends and enemies alike call him Volk—Russian for *wolf*. I consider myself to be both friend and enemy, so I call him Volk as well. It suits him in ways he's never understood.

Our *friend* Volk is a philanthropist of the highest order.

An art collector specializing in Renaissance paintings.

A shipping magnate worth four-point-seven billion dollars according to Forbes—though the actual number, buried in shell companies and offshore accounts, is closer to seven.

Friends with senators, oligarchs, and A-list celebrities.

Married twenty-eight years to a former ballerina who pretends not to know what he is.

Three grandchildren he bounces on his knee at charity galas while photographers capture his grandfatherly smile.

Our *enemy* Volk... well, he's the architect of the largest child trafficking operation in Eastern Europe.

The orphanages he funds aren't orphanages. They're Recruitment centers.

Those art acquisition trips to Prague, Budapest, Kyiv are sourcing missions.

His shipping empire doesn't move luxury goods across borders, it moves flesh.

Currently, Volk is naked and blindfolded. Steel cuffs around his wrists have him locked to the cage floor in absolute darkness about three miles from here.

The night-vision feed shows him testing the restraints again. Pulling at them methodically, intelligently.

Still believing this situation is salvageable.

That his lawyers, his political connections, his billions will extract him from this.

They won't.

I'll deal with him later.

The right wall of monitors holds my attention now.

Scarletta stepping off the Gulfstream onto Story Island's tarmac. She's still wearing my old Harvard t-shirt and black sweat pants.

The February sun is turning her hair gold as the Caribbean wind catches it, blowing it across her face. Not in some romantic, photogenic way, either. The gusts are whipping those dirty blonde strands so violently that she has to hold both sides of her head with her hands just to see where the hell she's going. Walking almost sideways down the stairs, squinting against the brightness after hours in the plane's dim cabin.

To call the vibe radiating off her body language *annoyed* would be a dramatic understatement.

She's pissed.

Genuinely, visibly pissed.

I can't help it—I snicker.

Her trip has been anything but relaxing. The invitation to the hunt directed her to go downstairs immediately upon receiving it, so she did—of course she did, eager little thing.

But I left her waiting for the limousine for nearly an hour in her apartment lobby. Just sitting there in my clothes, probably wondering if I'd forgotten about her entirely.

It was necessary, though. Cruel, yes, but necessary. I needed to arrive in the Caribbean before she did. Needed to be here, waiting, watching, in complete control of the infrastructure before her plane ever touched down.

Once she finally got to the FBO terminal at Idaho Falls Regional Airport, I had her plane grounded for two hours under the pretense of 'mechanical issues.' Some vague problem with the hydraulics that required a full inspection.

She sat in the private lounge—I watched her on the security cameras—pretending to read a magazine while internally spiraling with anxiety. Wondering if this was part of it. If I was testing her. If she should leave.

She didn't leave.

Which set the perfect tone for the 'normal not-normal turbulence' she experienced during the entire seven-hour flight. Nothing dangerous, of course. Nothing the pilots couldn't handle easily. But enough chop, enough sudden drops and jarring bumps to keep her white-knuckled and nauseous the whole way.

I specifically instructed them to take a route through some rough weather patterns. Make it memorable. Make her arrive already off-balance, already questioning whether she's made a terrible mistake.

Small games. Necessary delays. Minor psychological adjustments to ensure she arrives exactly as unsteady as I need her to be.

Control, I've learned, isn't just in the grand gestures—it's in the minutiae. The orchestration of a thousand tiny details that add up to total dominance before she even realizes the game has started.

She thinks she understands what this 'hunt' entails—they all do when they first arrive here, armed with their fantasies and half-formed expectations culled from fiction and forum posts.

But it's never the same chase twice. Every woman brings different fears, different desires, different breaking points.

The island itself shifts the dynamic—weather patterns, wildlife sounds, the particular quality of moonlight filtering through jungle canopy. So many variables to account for on Story Island. So many opportunities for improvisation within the carefully constructed framework.

I allow myself a small breath of satisfaction, settling deeper into my chair as I scan the array of monitors before me. Very pleased with how meticulously this particular event has been choreographed. Every contingency planned for, every potential complication anticipated and neutralized before it could manifest.

Volk's presence on the sister island two miles south of here is a distraction I could do without. His scales weren't due to be balanced until next week.

But adaptation is a hallmark of genius.

And I am nothing, if not a genius.

I adapted.

He's here, he'll be dealt with, the scales will balance, and Scarletta Mae Desmond will have a Valentine's Day experience she'll never forget.

I watch her squint against the harsh Caribbean sun, one hand still pressed against her windblown hair as a man in an impeccable linen suit materializes at the bottom of the aircraft stairs. He doesn't introduce himself. Doesn't offer pleasantries or small talk.

Just gestures toward the tree line where a narrow stone path disappears into the hibiscus hedges.

She follows.

Good girl.

I zoom in on camera three, tracking her progression along the winding trail. The path is deliberately disorienting—curves back on itself twice, creates the illusion of distance when the staging suite is only two hundred yards from the landing pad. Psychological preparation. By the time she arrives, she'll feel isolated, cut off, dependent on whoever's waiting inside.

The suited man motions towards the pavilion's entrance—there's no door, just a gap between two massive support columns—and steps aside.

Scarletta hesitates.

Then enters.

And there they are.

The same three male attendants who bathed her, oiled her, touched her seven weeks ago at the auction preparation.

I watch Scarletta's face on monitor six—the high-angle feed that captures her initial reaction. Her eyes widen slightly. Recognition, followed immediately by something that looks suspiciously like relief.

She knows them.

Which means she knows what's coming.

The dark-haired one steps forward first, taking both her hands in his, leaning in to kiss her cheek. "Welcome back, beautiful."

The blonde one moves to her other side, brushing his lips against her temple. "We've missed you."

The tall one slides his palm down her spine, fingers splaying across her lower back. "So good to see you again."

She's blushing. Hard. That telltale pink flush crawling up her throat, spreading across her cheeks.

But she doesn't pull away.

Doesn't demand answers or explanations the way she did last time, wide-eyed, and terrified, and stammering questions they refused to answer.

This time she just... lets them.

Stands there, breathing a little faster, while three sets of hands begin their work.

The dark-haired one reaches for the hem of my Harvard shirt and lifts it slowly over her head. Underneath, she's wearing a bra.

I lean forward, studying the monitor. Black lace. Delicate. Pretty.

The little slut.

I love it.

The blonde one kneels, hooking his fingers into the waistband of my sweatpants, dragging them down her thighs. She steps out of them obediently, and he runs his hands up her calves, over her knees, pausing at her thighs. He looks up at her with adoration.

Scarletta bites her lip.

Her black lace underwear matches the bra. What a good little slut.

The tall one slides the bra straps off her shoulders, trailing his fingertips along her collarbones. "May I?"

Scarletta nods automatically, then sucks in a breath.

He unclasps it, letting the black lace fall away.

Her nipples are already rock fucking hard.

I pull my cock out, wrapping my fist around the base.

This is going to be good.

They're not wasting time with the pretense of professional detachment—this time... they're *seducing her.*

The dark-haired one cups her breast, thumb circling her nipple, and she makes a small sound in the back of her throat —half gasp, half whimper—that goes straight to my dick.

The blonde one is still kneeling, pressing open-mouthed kisses to her inner thighs, inching higher.

The tall one moves behind her, wrapping one arm around her waist to hold her steady while his other hand slides down her stomach toward her black panties.

She's trembling.

Trying so fucking hard to control herself.

I can see it in the way she's clenching her jaw. The way her hands are fisted at her sides instead of reaching for them. The way she's staring at some fixed point on the far wall, refusing to look down at what they're doing to her body.

Fail, baby.

Give in.

Let them make you come.

I want to see it.

Want to see what you look like when you surrender to strangers touching you, pleasuring you, working you over like a team of professionals whose only job is getting you wet and desperate.

And then later—hours from now, when you're deep in the jungle thinking you've escaped me—I'll drag you back by your hair and punish you for it.

Spank that perfect ass until you're sobbing apologies for letting other men make you feel good.

Use your own weakness against you.

Make you beg for forgiveness while I fuck you so hard you forget your own name.

I'm not jealous.

Jealousy would imply I've lost control, that something's happening outside my orchestration, that she's choosing them over me.

None of that is true.

I told them exactly what to do to her. Where to touch. How to position her body so every camera angle captures her face, her hands, the moment she breaks.

I own this.

I own her.

I own every second of pleasure they're about to give her, because I'm the one who scripted it.

The dark-haired one pinches her nipple and she gasps, arching into his hand.

The blonde one hooks his fingers into her panties, dragging them down.

"Look at you," he whispers, running one finger through her folds. "Already so wet for us."

She whimpers.

The tall one's hand finds her other breast, kneading roughly while his mouth works against her neck.

They're coordinating beautifully—three sets of hands, three different sensations, overwhelming her nervous system until she can't think straight.

Can't resist.

Can't do anything but feel.

And then the dark-haired one guides her backward.

Toward the centerpiece of the staging suite.

The tub contraption.

I almost laugh watching her eyes go wide when she sees it.

It's a masterpiece of function and intimidation—custom-built hybrid of clawfoot soaking tub and gynecological examination table, carved from a single piece of black volcanic stone. The basin itself is deep enough for full-body submersion, five feet long and three wide. Polished smooth.

At the far end, hinged stirrups that fold up from the tub's edge. Polished steel. Leather padding. Locking ankle cuffs.

Medieval aesthetic meets clinical efficiency.

The participant is bathed, prepared, made vulnerable—then the water drains to knee-level, the stirrups deploy, and her legs are locked wide open for whatever comes next.

Shaving. Inspection. Penetration.

Complete access to her most intimate parts while she's helpless to close her thighs or hide herself.

Psychological torture dressed up as spa treatment.

They guide Scarletta toward it now, the dark-haired one supporting her elbow like she's stepping into something precious.

The water's already steaming, lavender and eucalyptus rising in fragrant clouds.

She looks back over her shoulder—not at them, but at the entrance.

Looking for me.

Wondering if I'm watching.

I am, baby.

I'm *always* watching.

CHAPTER 2
SCARLETTA

I'm naked again.

New place, same strangers. Same humiliating vulner-ability.

My three attendants guide me toward the tub and I try not to panic because *Jesus Christ,* it looks like something from a medieval torture museum.

Black stone. Cold and massive. Deep enough to drown in.

And at the far end—stirrups.

Stirrups.

Like the exam table. A moment from Christmas Eve flashes through my mind. The way my masked man guided my heels into the stirrups after he caught me. After he learned that I couldn't be trusted to be still so he had to strap me in. The look in his eyes behind that mask—god, it made me want him to do very sick, strange things to me.

But this gyno-tub… what the hell is it?

I'm trying to reconcile where I even am right now. The Caribbean, obviously. Tropical heat, palm trees, that thick humidity that makes my hair frizz instantly. But I don't actu-ally know. It's an island. I saw it from the window of the plane. Two of them, actually. Very close together. One with a lot of infrastructure, one without. But I could be anywhere. Mexico. Belize. Who knows.

The trip here was awful.

I waited almost an hour for the limo. Standing in the lobby of my apartment building, checking my phone every thirty seconds, convinced the masked man changed his mind. Convinced the whole invitation was a joke. *You really thought someone would pay fifty thousand dollars for you?*

When the car finally arrived, I almost didn't get in.

That's not true.

I was always going to get in.

The plane was delayed—mechanical issues, they said. I sat in that private terminal for another two hours, spiraling, convincing myself this was a sign. A cosmic intervention telling me to go home.

I didn't.

The flight itself was turbulent as hell. I felt sick the entire time. Gripping the armrests, stomach churning, convinced we'd crash into the ocean and no one would ever find me because I hadn't told anyone where I was going.

Who would I have told? My mother didn't even call me on Christmas this year. When I called her later in the afternoon on Christmas day,—still shaking, and excited, and confused, and happy, and bewildered, and relieved that my bank account held more digits than I'd ever thought possible in a single account balance—she made excuses for not calling me. Claimed she was traveling and didn't have service. As she was talking to me on the phone.

I didn't even push back. She's not worth the fight.

But my hesitations for this experience were real, even if I had no one to bounce them off of. The whole flight here I kept thinking I should tell the pilot to turn around. Demand it.

Didn't.

I kept thinking I was insane for coming. That this is proof I'm damaged beyond belief.

It is, too. I *am* insane. Absolutely unable to make a good decision if my fucking life depended on it, because I left the cameras up in my apartment.

All sixteen of them are still running. Still recording everything I do. I know exactly where they are now. The masked man told me how to disable them and I... just... didn't.

I didn't change my passwords, didn't remove the keystroke logger.

I *want* him watching me.

I want him reading every filthy word I type into *The Watcher*, the novel I'm writing about him. About us. About everything he did to me.

I want him to see that I kept his Harvard shirt.

That I touch myself thinking about him.

That I accepted this invitation the second I saw it because forty-eight hours with him is worth any amount of money, any amount of fear, any amount of—

"Easy," one of them murmurs, steadying my elbow as I step into the tub. The water's steaming. Lavender. Eucalyptus.

And then—hands. *Everywhere.*

One cups my breast immediately, soaping it with deliberate pressure that makes my nipples harden. Another slides down my stomach. The third is working shampoo into my hair, tilting my head back, exposing my throat.

Oh god.

I try to stay still. Try to breathe. Try to remember this is just preparation, just like before.

Except it's not like before.

Before, they were gentle. Clinical. Professional.

This time they're... aggressive.

The one at my breast pinches my nipple between soapy fingers, rolling it, watching my face for reaction. The one washing my stomach lets his hand drift lower. Lower.

Between my legs.

I gasp.

His fingers slide through my folds, not accidental, not incidental—deliberate. Circling my clit with expert precision while his other hand grips my hip to hold me steady.

He's watching.

The thought slams into me with absolute certainty.

My masked man is watching right now. Probably on a dozen screens. Probably stroking that massive cock of his while three strangers touch me in a bathtub built like a gynecological nightmare.

This is his fetish.

Voyeurism.

I've written about it in—god, how many stories? Twelve? Fifteen? The protagonist watched through hidden cameras, touched by strangers while her captor observes from somewhere else, getting off on her humiliation, her helplessness, her—

"Fuck," I whimper.

The attendant between my legs increases pressure. His thumb works my clit in tight circles while his fingers tease my entrance. Not penetrating. Just... threatening to.

The one at my breast leans in and whispers, "You're so wet, beautiful. We can feel it."

I am. God, I'm *dripping*. The water around my thighs probably has my arousal floating in it like some kind of sick evidence of exactly what I am.

A slut who gets wet when strangers touch her.

A broken girl who craves this.

I could come right now. Right this second. His thumb is in exactly the right spot, the right pressure, the right rhythm. My pussy is clenching around nothing, desperate, *begging* to be filled.

But I hold it.

Because I don't know what he wants.

Does he want me to come? To lose control in front of these men while he watches from wherever he is?

Or does he want me to be strong? To deny myself? To prove I'm saving myself for him?

I don't *know*.

The attendant washing my hair rinses it, his fingers massaging my scalp with firm, possessive strokes. The one at my breast soaps down my ribs, my stomach, my hips. The one between my legs—

His finger slides inside me.

Just one. Just to the first knuckle. But enough to make me gasp, and arch, and nearly come on the spot.

Then he withdraws.

The water starts draining. It quickly lowers to knee level, then stops with a weird *glug* sound. "What's happening?" I ask, trying to sit up and look around.

One of the men shushes me, pushing me so my back is resting against the stone tub.

A mechanical noise—then my hips begin to lift out of the tub. Again, I try and sit up. Trying to figure out what the hell is happening.

And again, the attendant gently—but firmly—pushes me back.

I'm lifted.

Not by hands—by the *tub itself*.

My hips rise out of the water with a mechanical *whirr* that sounds like something from a sci-fi horror movie. The stone beneath my lower back tilts up, up, up, raising my pelvis while the rest of me stays submerged to my ribs.

Then the stirrups swing wide.

Metallic clicks. One after another. *Click-click-click-click*— like some medieval gynecological Transformer unfolding for battle.

Oh my god.

What the actual fuck is this thing?

The blond attendant picks up my right foot with gentle

hands. His thumb strokes my ankle as he guides my heel into the stirrup. The metal is cold. Padded, but cold.

"Wait—" I try to pull back.

"Shh," he murmurs. "Just relax."

He closes something around my ankle. A cuff. Leather-lined but unmistakably a *restraint*. It locks with a soft *snick*.

My left foot goes next.

The dark-haired one guides it into position while I'm still processing what's happening. Another cuff. Another lock.

My legs are spread.

Wide.

Oh god.

The stirrups hold me open at an angle that makes my pussy completely exposed, raised above the waterline like I'm being presented for inspection. My thighs are trembling. I can feel cool air against my throbbing pussy, can feel how wet I am, how swollen.

I try to close my legs.

Can't.

The stirrups don't budge.

"Please—" I whisper.

The tall one with the long hair moves to my head, kneeling beside the tub. His hand cups my cheek. "You're okay, beautiful. Just breathe."

I'm breathing too fast. Panicking. Because I can't see what's happening down there. My head is low in the tub, water lapping at my shoulders, and my hips are raised up like—

Like an offering.

Like a sacrifice on some kind of stone altar.

The blond one moves between my spread legs, and that's when I see it.

The tray.

Shaving cream. Razor. Oil. Towels.

Oh no.

"We're going to make you perfect for him," the blond says, his voice so gentle it makes my stomach clench. "Just relax and let us work."

I want to protest. Want to tell them—

The shaving cream is warm.

The blond one spreads it along my bikini line with his bare fingers, working it into my skin with slow, deliberate strokes. His thumb brushes my clit—accidental or intentional, I don't know—and I gasp.

"Easy," the tall one murmurs from behind my head. His hands are in my hair now, massaging my scalp, tilting my head back. "Just feel it. Don't fight."

The third attendant—the dark-haired one—moves to my breast. His soapy hand cups it, thumb circling my nipple until it's hard and aching.

I close my eyes.

Because I can't watch this. Can't process it. Can't reconcile what's happening with who I'm supposed to be.

Good girls don't get wet when strangers shave their pussy.

Good girls don't arch into the touch when fingers pinch their nipples.

Good girls don't—

"He's watching you right now, beautiful."

My eyes snap open.

The tall one is looking down at me, his fingers still working through my wet hair. "Your masked man. He's watching. Put on a good show for him."

Oh god.

The razor glides along my bikini line. Smooth, efficient, careful. The blond one works with clinical precision, one hand spreading my skin taut while the other guides the blade.

I feel every stroke.

Every deliberate scrape of metal against my most vulnerable places.

"He told us you write stories like this," the tall one continues, his voice low and intimate. "Pretend you're her. Pretend you're Jasmine in *Mine, All Mine*."

My breath catches.

He's right.

I *did* write about this.

Not this exact contraption—god, nothing this elaborate—but the fantasy was the same. Jasmine in her master's bathing chamber. Black stone tub. Three male servants preparing her for inspection. Shaving her, oiling her, making her perfect while her master watched from behind a screen.

He's still doing it.

The masked man is still tailoring my experience using my own words. My own darkest fantasies.

Really, really intense experiences—but familiar. Things I've written about. Things I've already processed and survived on the page.

He's giving me a reference point.

And somehow... somehow that makes it less terrifying.

He *sees* me.

Not just my body. Not just my willingness to be here.

He sees the *writer*. The woman who processes life through fiction. Who needs narrative structure to make sense of chaos.

"Good girl," the blond one murmurs. "So good for us."

His hand spreads more shaving cream. Lower this time. Between my pussy lips.

I whimper.

Because he's touching me there. Deliberately. His fingers work the cream along my labia, making sure every inch is covered, and I can feel myself getting wetter, feel my clit throbbing, feel my pussy clenching on nothing.

"Enjoy it," the tall one whispers near my ear. "He wants you to enjoy this."

The razor glides along my outer lips. Slow. Careful. The

blond one's other hand cups my ass, tilting my hips for better access.

The dark-haired one at my breast pinches my nipple hard.

I gasp.

"That's it," he murmurs. "Let him hear you."

The masked man is watching right now—probably stroking his cock, probably getting off on how spread open I am, how helpless, how three strangers are touching me and I can't do anything but take it.

The razor moves lower.

Between my ass cheeks.

Oh god.

I try to stay still. Try to breathe. Try not to think about how exposed I am right now, how violated, how—

"Almost done," the blond one says. "You're doing so well."

He rinses me with warm water from a pitcher. The liquid cascades over my freshly shaved skin, washing away the last of the cream.

Then oil.

His hands spread it everywhere. Along my bikini line, between my pussy lips, over my ass. Massaging it in with firm, possessive strokes that make me shake.

The dark-haired one's hand slides from my breast to my stomach. Down. Down.

His fingers find my clit.

"*Fuck,*" I whimper.

"Should she come?" the blond one asks, looking up at the tall one.

The tall one smiles. "I think she needs to."

No.

I can't.

If I come now, he'll—

The masked man will—

But the dark-haired one's fingers are circling my clit with expert precision. The blond one's hands are spreading my pussy lips, holding me open, exposing everything. The tall one is whispering in my ear about how wet I am, how good I look, how my masked man is watching me lose control.

I try to hold it.

Try to be strong.

Try to—

The dark-haired one slides two fingers inside me.

Deep.

Curling up to hit that spot that makes my vision white out.

I come.

Hard.

My pussy clenches around his fingers, my back arches against the stone tub, and I scream. Actually *scream*. The sound echoes off the pavilion ceiling, raw, and desperate, and proof of exactly what I am.

A good little slut who comes when strangers finger her.

The orgasm rolls through me in waves. Violent. Consuming. His fingers don't stop—they keep working that spot inside me while his thumb presses my clit, milking every last spasm from my body.

When I finally go limp, gasping, the tall one pets my hair.

"Good girl," he whispers. "He's going to punish you so badly for that."

My eyes snap open.

What?

The dark-haired one withdraws his fingers slowly. "That's how it ended for Jasmine, wasn't it?"

Oh no.

Oh god.

He's right.

In *Mine, All Mine*, Jasmine came during her preparation. Her master had explicitly forbidden it—told her to save herself for him—but she couldn't resist. The servants touched her and she failed the test.

So he punished her.

Whipped her.

Edged her for hours without letting her come again.

Made her beg, and cry, and confess how weak she was.

I understand now.

The masked man *wanted* me to come. Set me up to fail. Orchestrated this entire scene knowing I wouldn't be able to resist three sets of hands, knowing my body would betray me.

Just like Jasmine.

So he could punish me for it.

The stirrups unlock with metallic clicks. My legs lower slowly, the mechanical tub returning me to a normal bathing position.

"Time to get you ready for the hunt," the blond one says, offering his hand to help me stand.

My legs are shaking.

My pussy is still throbbing.

And somewhere, I know the masked man is watching with that predatory smile I can't see, but can always feel.

CHAPTER 3
CALEB

My hand freezes mid-stroke. Cock still slick. Come cooling on my knuckles.

Scarletta just handed me everything.

She came for them. Surrendered to their fingers, their mouths, their coordinated assault on her self-control. Exactly like Jasmine in her story. Exactly like I knew she would.

Permission granted.

I'm going to make her scream.

Not from pleasure this time. From pain. From the flat crack of my palm across her ass, from the sting of leather against her thighs, from the humiliation of being spanked like a disobedient child in front of cameras she knows are watching.

Station One isn't just a test of courage. It's a punishment platform. Sixty feet up, suspended in open air, nowhere to hide when I stripe her skin red.

I grab the warm towel from beneath the silver dome—always prepared, always three steps ahead—and clean myself with efficient strokes. My eyes never leave the center screen where the dark-haired one hands Scarletta a small cream-colored envelope sealed with black wax.

She takes it with shaking fingers.

Still wrapped in white silk. Still dripping from the bath. Still swollen and sensitive from the orgasm she shouldn't have taken.

The attendants step back. One. Two. Three synchronized steps into shadow.

Then gone.

Scarletta looks up. Turns. Her eyes scan the empty pavilion, searching for the men who just violated every inch of her freshly shaved pussy.

No one.

Just her. The envelope. And sixteen hidden cameras capturing the confusion spreading across her face.

She breaks the wax seal. Unfolds the card. Starts reading.

I watch her lips move silently, forming the words I spent an hour perfecting last night.

Roses are red, Violets are blue...

Her face flushes. Shame or arousal—doesn't matter. Both feed what's coming.

You came for those strangers, Now you'll pay what's due.

She bites her lower lip. The same nervous tell she's had since I started watching her six months ago. When she's scared but turned on. When her body wants what her mind refuses.

Her thighs press together. Subtle. Unconscious. She's already wet again.

My good little slut got her pussy all wet
While hands that weren't mine made her moan.
You earned yourself punishment—don't you forget:
Every orgasm you have should be mine alone.

She reads faster now. Eyes skipping ahead, hungry for information, desperate to know what I've planned.

Walk north through the jungle, 1.2 miles precise,
You'll find the tall tree with rope hanging down.
Climb to the platform (don't think twice),

Cuff yourself up there and wait for your crown.

Her breathing changes. Shallow. Quick. Fear response activating.

The bonus is five thousand if you're brave enough, dear,
But the real reward's the pain I'll deliver.
You let them touch you—now face your fear:
Heights, and my hands, and the way you will quiver.

She touches her throat. Another tell. When reality exceeds fantasy. When the game becomes real.

Strip off that robe before you begin.
Take only this map and the watch on your wrist.
You have two hours to arrive, my sweet sin,
Or forfeit all bonuses—you get the gist.

Her eyes snap back to the top of the card. Rereading. Confirming she understood correctly.

Yes, Scarletta. Naked. Through the jungle. Because I want you vulnerable. Exposed. Unable to hide behind fabric when branches scrape your skin and humidity makes you sweat.

She flips the card over. Finds the map I printed—detailed topographic lines marking elevation changes, creek crossings, the precise GPS coordinates of Station One.

One final rule before we begin:
You're mine now—every breath, every sin.
I'm watching each step through the jungle you take.
Quit on me now, and see what I break.

She looks up. Not at any specific camera. Just up. Knowing I'm everywhere and nowhere.

"Fuck," she whispers.

The microphones catch it. Clean. Clear.

Now go.

She stands frozen for thirty-seven seconds. I count them. Watch her chest rise and fall. Watch her fingers clench the card hard enough to crumple the edges.

Then she unties the silk robe and lets it fall to the ground at her feet.

For a moment, she just stands there naked in the pavilion's dappled sunlight. Beautiful, and vulnerable, and... mine.

Then she picks up the tracker watch from the small table beside her, straps it onto her wrist, and jumps a little when it beeps.

1:59:59.

1:59:58.

She clutches the card in her hand, takes one last look around the empty pavilion, and then walks toward the north entrance.

Barefoot.

Naked.

And most certainly afraid.

The jungle swallows her in three strides.

I switch to the left wall. Sixteen monitors showing Chaff Island.

Volk's cage sits in a clearing two miles inland from the drop zone. Steel bars. Concrete floor. No roof—just open sky and the oppressive heat of Caribbean sun beating down on naked skin.

The drone hovers above him, a tether holding his instructions dangling from it. Cream envelope. Black wax seal. Identical to Scarletta's except for one critical detail.

Hers has roses and promises of punishment that will make her scream while I coax blissful orgasms out of her.

His has a death sentence with a sixty-minute head start.

I zoom Camera 3 closer as the drone drops the card. It flutters down in a spiral. Volk reaches up, fumbles, grasps it with desperation.

Opens it, eyes searching for salvation...

You want to survive? Then listen close, prey.

His hands shake. Slight tremor. Barely visible. But I see everything.

I'll give you one chance to get away.

He thinks I'm bluffing. That this is some elaborate black-mail scheme. That I want money, or leverage, or information.

He's wrong.

I want his screams.

Move east through the jungle, one mile straight— Station One holds your freedom. Don't be late.

It's a lie, of course. He's here now. He's never leaving. Not alive, anyway.

You have sixty minutes to reach the cache,
Where clothes and supplies and weapons stash.
Miss the deadline and I hunt you bare,
Naked and screaming through island air.
I'll start with your fingers, peel back the nails,
Then move to your cock while you beg and you wail.
I'll skin you alive and keep you awake,
Feed you your own flesh for every mistake.
Now run.

Volk hesitates, frozen in place, his chest heaving with ragged breaths. He tilts his head back, squinting against the harsh morning sun as he searches the empty sky. The drone is already gone—vanished as quickly as it appeared—but he stares upward anyway, as if divine intervention might materialize from the cloudless expanse above him.

Water. That's what his cracked lips are begging for. Sixteen hours on this godforsaken rock without a single drop. His throat must feel like sandpaper by now.

Food would be a fever dream at this point. His body's already eating itself from the inside.

But I give him nothing.

Not a goddamn thing.

Because nothing is precisely what he's earned after all these years. Less than nothing, if such a thing existed.

The beauty of it—the exquisite perfection of his unhap-pily-ever-after—is that I don't even need to set foot on Chaff Island for this hunt to reach its inevitable conclusion.

Every trap, every failsafe, every agonizing checkpoint I've designed will execute flawlessly without my physical presence.

The island itself has become my instrument of justice.

It's engineered to kill him methodically, systematically—one excruciating failure at a time—until his body finally gives out or his mind shatters completely.

A very slow death.

A very painful death.

An *excruciating* death.

Exactly what he deserves.

He earned it.

I switch back to the right wall. Scarletta's only made it a hundred feet into the jungle and she's already miserable.

Good.

Camera 4 captures her swatting frantically at the air around her head. Something buzzed too close to her ear. She flinches, slaps at her shoulder, examines her palm for evidence of the kill.

Nothing there.

"Fuck," she mutters, then louder: "Fuck, fuck, fuck."

She's hopping now, lifting one foot then the other off the path. The ground's not smooth here—volcanic rock worn down over millennia but still rough enough to hurt tender feet that have spent twenty-two years in sneakers and socks.

A mosquito lands on her breast. She notices it, watches it probe her skin, then smacks herself hard enough to leave a red mark.

I don't feel sorry for her.

Not even a little.

The bug population on Story Island is a fraction of what Volk's experiencing right now on Chaff. I've spent three years and half a million dollars making sure my clients—wealthy men paying premium rates for fantasy fulfillment—don't spend their forty-eight hours swatting mosquitoes instead of fucking their willing participants.

Wildlife management wasn't something I considered when I first bought this place. Thought the "authentic jungle experience" would add to the appeal. Took exactly one hunt to learn otherwise.

So I brought in experts. Environmental consultants who specialized in luxury eco-resorts. Pest control specialists with experience in Caribbean properties. Even a goddamn ornithologist from Cornell.

The solution was elegant. Natural. Self-sustaining.

Guinea fowl.

I released thirty birds three years ago. Semi-domesticated flock imported from a breeding facility in Jamaica. They adapted immediately, roosting in the trees near the resort compound, patrolling the jungle paths like they'd been doing it their entire lives.

Now there are a hundred and fifty of them.

Maybe more—they breed faster than I track.

Loud as hell. Their calls echo through the jungle at dawn and dusk, sharp and grating. But effective.

They eat everything. Ticks, mosquitoes, centipedes, scorpions. And snakes—Christ, they're vicious with snakes. I've watched them mob a fer-de-lance, pecking and clawing until it's shredded meat.

The trails Scarletta's walking right now are relatively safe. The guinea fowl clear them daily, hunting for insects and small reptiles. She might see one or two snakes if she's unlucky, but they'll be small, non-venomous, already fleeing from the birds' territories.

Still doesn't stop her from muttering about them.

"Please no snakes, please no snakes, please—"

Camera 5 picks up her voice as she climbs over a moss-covered boulder. Her bare pussy flashes in the sunlight filtering through the canopy. Freshly shaved. Glistening with sweat already.

She lands hard on the other side, stumbles, catches herself against a tree trunk.

Then freezes.

Her eyes lock on something in the underbrush.

A gecko. Six inches long, bright green, completely harmless.

It blinks at her.

She screams and runs.

I laugh. Actually laugh. First genuine amusement I've felt in weeks.

She makes it another fifty feet before slowing down, chest heaving, looking back over her shoulder to confirm the lizard didn't chase her.

The jungle's not that dangerous. Not on Story Island.

I've cultivated this place carefully. Every hundred yards along the marked trails, there's a bug zapper—solar-powered units mounted in trees, designed to look like birdhouses from a distance. They hum quietly, drawing mosquitoes and gnats away from the paths.

Citronella torches at each station. Natural repellent plants —lemongrass, marigolds, basil—cultivated in strategic clusters near the pavilion and rest areas.

The staging pavilion where the attendants prepared her has a fine mesh screening it from fifty yards out. Looks like open air from inside, but it's basically like a pool lanai, only much bigger. There is one open end—the path that leads to Station 1. So some bugs do get in, but not many.

Luxury wilderness.

That's the aesthetic I maintain.

Clients pay for psychological intensity, not tropical diseases.

Scarletta stops walking. Bends forward, hands on her

knees, breathing hard. She's only covered maybe two hundred feet total. Has another mile to go.

The tracker watch on her wrist beeps.

1:54:12.

She looks at it. Realizes how much time she's already wasted. Straightens up, wipes sweat from her forehead with the back of her hand, and keeps moving.

Slower now. More careful. Watching where she steps.

Smart girl.

Camera 6 shows her approaching the first creek crossing. Fifteen feet wide, knee-deep, crystal clear water running over smooth stones. I had this entire stream bed cleared and sanitized. No sharp rocks, no leeches, no parasites.

She stands at the edge, staring down at the water like it might be acid.

"It's just water," she whispers to herself. "Just fucking water."

But she's thinking about what's in it. What might be in it. Bacteria, parasites, things that could crawl up inside her while she's wading across.

She's not wrong to worry.

On Chaff Island, the water's filthy. Stagnant pools breeding grounds for dengue and malaria. Volk will have to drink it eventually, or die of dehydration. Either choice kills him, just at different speeds.

The water here on Story Island is filtered through volcanic rock, tested weekly by my staff, and treated with UV purification systems hidden upstream.

Scarletta could drink straight from this creek and be fine.

But she doesn't know that.

She steps in slowly. Gasps at the temperature—it's cold, fed by underground springs—and picks her way across with exaggerated care.

Halfway through, something brushes her ankle.

She shrieks, flails, almost falls.

Just a leaf. Carried by the current.

She makes it to the far bank and collapses on the moss, breathing like she just sprinted a marathon.

1:51:33.

"Get up," I say out loud, even though she can't hear me. "You're wasting time."

But she doesn't get up. She lies there on her back, naked and panting, staring up at the canopy.

A guinea fowl crashes through the underbrush twenty feet from her position.

She bolts upright, eyes wide.

The bird emerges onto the path. Speckled grey and white, about the size of a small chicken, with a distinctive helmet-like crest on its head.

It looks at her.

She looks at it.

"Nice bird," she whispers. "Good bird. Don't... peck me."

The guinea fowl clucks—low, rattling sound—and waddles past her into the jungle on the other side of the creek.

Scarletta watches it disappear, then looks down at the tracker.

1:50:18.

"Shit."

She gets to her feet. Brushes moss off her ass. Picks up her crumpled card from where she dropped it, checks the map. Checks her watch. Looks around orienting herself.

Ah, she's figured out there's a compass on there.

She starts walking. Faster now. Finally understanding that time is the real enemy here, not the jungle.

She thinks she's in control of what happens. That her pace can change the outcome. That her compliance, or failure will dictate... *anything*.

It can't. It won't.

I've planned for every fucking possible scenario.

The whole point of this island is... her *enjoyment*.

CHAPTER 4
SCARLETTA

The watch beeps.

I freeze mid-step, certain I've failed—certain he's going to punish me harder because I'm late, because I'm slow, because I'm *me*—but the timer reads 0:02:17.

Two minutes.

I made it with two fucking minutes to spare.

The clearing opens up in front of me like something out of a fever dream. Or maybe I actually *have* fever. Malaria. Dengue. Whatever tropical nightmare is currently incubating in my bloodstream because I walked through a goddamn jungle naked and barefoot like some sort of feral idiot.

There's a massive tree in the center. Ancient. Gnarled. The kind of tree that looks like it's been here since before humans invented fire, waiting patiently to murder someone.

Thick vines wrap around the trunk like veins. The branches spread out overhead in this twisted canopy that blocks most of the light, turning the clearing dim and greenish and *wrong*. Like a fairy tale forest where children get eaten.

A rope ladder hangs down from somewhere high up in the branches.

Next to it, an envelope dangles from a nail hammered into the bark.

Of course there's another fucking envelope.

I stumble forward, every nerve ending screaming. My feet are bleeding—I can feel it, even if I can't see it through the dirt caked on my skin. Something bit my shoulder. Or maybe scratched me. I don't know. Everything itches. *Everything.* Like ants are crawling under my skin, burrowing into my pores, laying eggs in my—

Stop.

I rip the envelope off the tree. My hands shake so badly I almost drop it.

Inside, another card. Another stupid goddamn poem written in his perfect handwriting.

My naughty little Valentine let strangers make her moan,
So sixty feet above the ground, she'll pay for what she's sown.
Climb the rope into the tree and prove you can obey—
Walk the plank, retrieve your cuffs, and give that ass away.
Walk back to the beam you started on, then face it like my whore,
Bend yourself across the wood and wait for what's in store.

"Fuck you."

I say it out loud. To the tree. To him. To the cameras I know are watching.

"Fuck. *You.*"

My voice cracks on the second word.

I look up.

Sixty feet.

Sixty fucking feet.

There's a platform up there. I can barely see it through the branches, but it's there—wooden planks lashed together, extending out from the trunk like a diving board suspended in nightmare territory.

I'm afraid of heights.

Like, *genuinely* afraid. The kind of afraid where I can't even stand near the railing on a second-floor balcony without my legs turning to jelly. The kind where I once had a panic attack in a glass elevator and had to take the stairs for the rest of the week.

And he wants me to climb sixty feet up a rope ladder.

Then walk out onto a plank.

Suspended in the air.

Above a jungle.

Naked.

I can't. I can't do this. It's not *possible*. I'm not capable of this. It's not within my abilities. I'm not—I don't have the capacity for this. I'm not the kind of person who climbs trees. I'm not athletic. I barely leave my apartment. I'm the girl who gets winded walking up four flights of stairs.

Climbing sixty feet up into a tree isn't in my... my... *constitution*.

Constitution? What the hell, Scarletta? The word floats through my panicked brain like it's auditioning for a role it doesn't deserve. It's not in my constitution. My fucking *constitution*.

Who even says that? What am I, some regency-era damsel clutching her pearls? Some fantasy princess fainting onto a chaise lounge because the prospect of physical exertion is too vulgar to contemplate?

Christ. I sound ridiculous. I sound like I'm writing dialogue for a character I'd mock in someone else's manuscript.

Oh, my God. I'm spiraling. I need to chill. Zen. Calm...

This is... safe. It has to be. I crane my neck back, squinting up through the canopy at the distant platform—barely visible through layers of leaves and dappled sunlight. The wood up there looks thick. Solid. Sturdy, even from this impossible distance.

Don't think about how far away it actually is. Don't think about how you can't possibly assess its structural integrity from sixty goddamn feet below. This is the masked man we're talking about here. Control freak extraordinaire. The man who orchestrated an entire auction, who rigged every detail of my arrival, who probably has backup plans for his backup plans.

He's obsessive. Meticulous. Pathologically thorough.

It's got to be safe. It has to be. He wouldn't put me in actual danger—not the kind that involves plummeting to my death from a tree platform in the middle of the jungle.

Right?

I take a breath and hold it as I read the poem again. Slower this time.

Bend yourself across the wood and wait for what's in store.

He's going to spank me.

He's going to make me climb up there, restrain myself, and then he's going to—

My pussy clenches.

Oh god.

I picture it. His hand coming down hard on my bare ass while I'm bent over a beam sixty feet in the air, helpless and exposed and completely at his mercy. Will he use his palm? A crop? That leather paddle I wrote about in *Prey*?

Will he make it hurt?

Or will he alternate—pain and pleasure, the way he did at the mansion when he spanked me and fingered me at the same time until I didn't know which sensation to focus on, until my brain short-circuited and I came so hard I *blacked out*?

I watched that footage so many times.

Sitting in my glamping tent, wearing his Harvard shirt, laptop balanced on my knees. I'd replay the part where he straps me to the exam table. The part where he makes me recite my own story while fucking me with a pen and his fingers. The part where I squirt for the first time in my life and sob afterward because I didn't know my body could do that.

I watched it until I memorized every angle. Every camera view. The way my face looked when I came. The way his masked face looked when he watched me fall apart.

I want him to touch me like that again.

I *need* him to.

Even if it means climbing this nightmare tree.

Even if it means I might actually die of a heart attack halfway up.

I grab the rope ladder.

It swings under my weight, unstable and terrifying, but I don't let go.

One rung. Then another.

My arms shake. My legs shake. Everything shakes.

The ground falls away beneath me and my stomach lurches but I keep climbing because if I stop I'll think about how high I am, and if I think about it I'll freeze, and if I freeze I'll fall and—

Don't look down. Don't look down. *Don't look fucking down.*

I look down.

The clearing is so far away it doesn't even look real anymore. Just green blur and shadows and *oh god oh god oh god*—

Keep climbing.

Rung, after rung, after rung.

My palms are slick with sweat. The rope burns against my skin. My thighs tremble with the effort of keeping myself steady.

When I finally haul myself over the edge of the platform, I collapse face-down on the wood, gasping.

The planks are warm under my cheek. Rough. Real.

I made it.

I'm not dead.

Yet.

When I can breathe again, I lift my head.

There's a narrow plank extending out from the main platform—maybe eight feet long, two feet wide. At the end, a wooden box with a latch.

Behind me, closer to the trunk, a thick beam mounted horizontally between two branches. Sturdy. Waist-height. With metal eyebolts screwed into the wood on either side.

I know exactly what those are for.

Next to the beam, another card.

Of course.

I crawl over—I'm not standing up, fuck that, I'm staying as low as possible—and read it.

Walk the plank. Retrieve your restraints. Return to the beam. Bend over it. Secure your right ankle to the eyebolt on the right. Secure your left wrist to the eyebolt on the left. Wait for your Master.

My hands won't stop shaking.

I look at the plank.

Then at the box.

Then down at the ground, which is so far away I can barely process the distance.

He wants me to walk out there.

Over open air.

To get handcuffs.

So I can restrain *myself.*

And wait for him to come punish me.

I crawl to the edge of the plank. Test it with one hand. It doesn't move. Solid. Bolted down, probably. Safe.

Probably.

He never said I had to stand. Well, walk the plank kind of implies it. But there was no rule against crawling.

Don't look down.

I let out a breath and inch forward.

You're not going to fall.

I make it to the box. Flip the latch. Inside there are black leather cuffs lined with soft padding.

I grab them, turn around, drop to my knees, and crawl slowly back across the plank. A bird flies through the trees, scaring the fuck out of me, and I wobble. My fingers grip the plank tight.

Calm down, Scarletta. You're three feet away. Three feet away...

I hold my breath, gripping the wood so tight, I can feel the splinters breaking my skin. But slowly, I cross that last bit of distance and reach the beam.

I blow out a breath... this is it.

The moment where I can still choose to climb back down. To walk away. To say *no, this is insane, I'm not doing this.*

But I don't want to walk away.

I want to bend over this beam and wait for him.

I want to feel his hand on my ass. His voice in my ear. His control wrapping around me like a second skin.

I want to surrender.

I buckle the right ankle cuff around myself first. Clip it to the eyebolt. Test the hold.

Secure.

Then I bend forward over the beam, the wood pressing against my stomach, my ass lifted and exposed to the open air.

To the cameras.

To him.

I reach back with my left hand and buckle the wrist cuff. Stretch my arm to clip it to the second eyebolt.

The lock clicks into place.

I'm trapped.

Restrained. Helpless. Waiting.

Exactly where he wants me.

My pussy throbs.

...

Nothing happens.

Chill, Scarletta. Chill. You literally just got here. It's been like thirty seconds.

...

Still nothing.

I've got a good look at the ground now. It's literally all I can see with the one eye that's not pressed against the bench.

A little chicken bird walks past, pecking at things.

A butterfly floats by.

Time slows.

Drags.

The... what's that? Something is moving through the trees.

Oh, shit. There he is. Holy fuck. He took his mask off. He's not wearing...

He looks up.

I lift my free hand to my mouth and bite the back of it. My *god*. He's actually fucking hot. I mean, I could tell he was hot. Even under the mask. But seeing it for the—

"There's my good little slut," he calls.

My pussy clenches just from his voice.

"I'll be right there, you naughty whore. Stay wet for me."

Oh, I'm wet all right. I'm fucking wet.

He disappears under the leaves and branches, but I can hear him climbing up. He gets here fast, like he climbs rope ladders for funsies.

And then... he's behind me.

I'm suddenly *dying* for him. For this touch. For his fingers, his hands, his cock, everything. I want all of him, right now.

His hand wraps around my throat from behind—not choking, just *holding*—and my entire body goes still.

Prey response. Frozen. Waiting.

His other hand slides between my legs.

I'm so wet his fingers glide through my folds without resistance. Zero friction. Just slick, humiliating evidence of how badly I want this.

"Jesus Christ," he mutters. "You're fucking soaked."

I bite down on my free hand again.

His thumb circles my clit—slow, deliberate—and I make

this pathetic whimpering sound that echoes across the clearing sixty feet below us.

"Do you have any idea how beautiful you look like this?" His voice is low. Rough. "Bent over. Restrained. Waiting for me to punish you."

I can't answer. Can't think. His fingers are doing things that make my brain shut down.

"But you were very, very bad, weren't you?"

His thumb presses harder against my clit and I gasp.

"Those men touched you. Put their hands all over this pretty body." His grip tightens on my throat. "Made you come."

Oh god.

"This body belongs to me. Not them. *Me.*"

His fingers push inside—two at once—and I cry out.

"Say it."

I don't understand what he wants. My mind is fog and need and the feeling of his fingers curling inside me.

"Say you belong to me."

"I—" My voice breaks. "I belong to you."

"Say you're mine."

"I'm yours."

"Again."

"I'm yours. I'm—fuck—I'm yours."

He pulls his fingers out and I actually *whine* at the loss.

Then his hand comes down on my ass.

Hard.

The sound cracks through the air like a gunshot and pain explodes across my skin—sharp, bright, *searing*—and I scream.

Holy *shit.*

That hurt.

That actually fucking hurt.

But underneath the pain: pleasure. Deep, throbbing,

impossible pleasure radiating from where his palm connected with my flesh.

My pussy clenches around nothing.

"Count them," he says.

Another strike. Harder this time.

I can't breathe. Can't think. The pain is—it's too much and not enough and—

"*Count.*"

"Two!" I gasp it out. "Two."

His hand comes down again. Same spot. Building heat on top of heat.

"Three!"

Again.

"Four!"

The pain is climbing now. Stacking. Each strike landing on already tender skin, amplifying the hurt until I'm sobbing into my arm.

But I'm also grinding against the beam. Desperate. Needy. My hips moving on their own, seeking friction that isn't there.

Five. Six. Seven.

I lose count somewhere around twelve.

Everything blurs together—pain and pleasure and the sound of his palm against my ass and my own voice crying out numbers that might be wrong but I don't care anymore because *oh god oh god oh god*—

He stops.

His fingers slide between my legs again, finding my clit, and I nearly come on the spot.

"Don't you dare," he warns.

I freeze.

His fingers circle. Press. Tease.

"You don't get to come until I say you can."

I'm shaking. My entire body trembling with the effort of holding back.

"Please." The word rips out of me. "Please, I need—"

"I know what you need."

His fingers push inside me again. Three this time. Stretching me. Filling me.

"You need to be fucked. Used. Owned."

He pumps his fingers slowly. Too slowly.

"You need someone who understands exactly how filthy you are."

I'm panting. Desperate.

"Someone who knows you write about being watched while you masturbate. About strangers touching you. About being punished for coming without permission."

His thumb finds my clit again and I nearly sob.

"Someone who's read every single one of your stories and knows that what you really want—what you've *always* wanted—is to be completely powerless."

I can feel it building. That edge. That cliff I'm about to fall over whether I have permission or not.

"Don't come," he says again.

His fingers curl inside me, hitting that spot that makes my vision go white, and I bite down on my hand so hard I taste blood.

"Good girl. Hold it."

Another spank. Hard. Right on my already burning ass.

I scream.

His fingers don't stop. They keep working. Keep pushing me higher.

Another strike.

Another.

The pain and pleasure merge into something I don't have words for. Something that makes me feel like I'm fracturing apart and being rebuilt all at once.

"Please." I'm begging now. Full-on begging. "Please let me come. Please. I can't—I need—"

"Not yet."

His fingers pump faster. Harder.

My orgasm hovers right there—*right fucking there*—and he won't let me have it.

Spank. Spank. Spank.

"Please!" I'm sobbing now. Actual tears streaming down my face. "Please, Master, please—"

He leans over me. His chest presses against my back.

His mouth right next to my ear.

"Beg me properly."

I don't even know what that means. I'm too far gone. Too desperate.

"Please let your slut come," I gasp. "Please, I need it, I'll do anything, please just let me—"

"No."

His fingers withdraw completely.

I make this sound—this broken, desperate, *animal* sound—because he just took everything away and left me dangling on the edge with nothing to push me over.

"You come when I decide you've earned it."

Another spank. Brutal this time.

My ass is on fire. Every nerve ending screaming.

But my pussy is still throbbing. Still desperate. Still *needing*.

His fingers return. Slower now. Teasing.

"Count for me again. From one. And this time, thank me after each number."

Oh god.

His hand comes down.

"One! Thank you, Master."

Again.

"Two! Thank you, Master."

The rhythm builds. His hand. His fingers. My voice counting and thanking and breaking apart with each strike.

"Ten! Thank you, Master!"

His fingers slide through my wetness—so much wetness I

can hear it, slick and obscene—and circle my clit with maddening lightness.

"You're dripping all over my hand," he says. "Making such a mess."

I am. I know I am. I can feel it running down my thighs.

"Filthy little slut."

His fingers push inside again. Deep. Curling.

"Don't come."

I'm dying. Actually dying. This is how I die—sixty feet up in a tree, restrained and desperate and so close to orgasm I can't see straight.

"Please." It's barely a whisper now. "Please, I can't—I can't hold it—"

"Yes, you can."

Another spank.

Another.

His fingers work faster. Harder. Relentless.

"Hold it."

I'm breaking. I can feel it happening. The part of me that's still trying to maintain control, still trying to be *good*—it's shattering.

"Please let me come. Please. I'm begging you. I'll do anything. *Anything*."

"Anything?"

"Yes! Yes, anything, just please—"

His fingers stop moving.

Still inside me.

Not moving.

"Then prove you can obey me first."

CHAPTER 5
CALEB

I've got Scarletta Mae Desmond exactly where I want her.

Trembling. Soaked. Desperate enough to promise anything if I'll just let her come.

But I won't.

Not here. Not at Station One.

She needs to understand what this hunt actually is. She doesn't get relief just because she begs prettily. Her body belongs to me completely—including her orgasms.

I withdraw my fingers slowly. Deliberately. Dragging them through her folds one last time before pulling out entirely.

Her reaction is immediate. A broken whimper, that turns into a moan, that turns into frantic writhing against the beam. Her restrained wrist pulls at the cuff. Her secured ankle strains against the leather.

"No—wait—please don't—"

I wipe my hand on her ass. Marking her with her own wetness.

"Are you leaving?" Her voice cracks. "Please don't leave me like this—"

I stand, step back, and watch her try to twist around to see me despite the restraints keeping her bent and exposed.

"Master, please—"

The panic in her voice makes my cock throb.

She genuinely thinks I might just walk away. Leave her edged, and desperate, and tied to this beam sixty feet off the ground.

I'm not that cruel.

Well. Not yet.

"I need—you can't just—" She's gasping now. "Please, I'm sorry, whatever I did wrong I'm sorry—"

"You didn't do anything wrong."

I crouch beside her. Run my hand down her spine.

She arches into the touch like she's starving for it.

"Then why—"

"Because you don't come until I decide you've earned it." I lean closer. "And you haven't earned it yet."

Her breath hitches.

"But I did everything—I climbed up here, I put the cuffs on, I took the spanking, I didn't come even though—"

"I know."

My fingers trace idle, wandering patterns on her lower back—slow circles, figure eights, random swirls that make her muscles flutter and twitch beneath my touch. Light enough to tease every nerve ending still screaming for release. Not nearly enough pressure to satisfy the desperate ache I've built inside her.

Each stroke deliberate. Calculated to keep her simmering right at the edge of madness.

"You've been very good," I murmur, letting genuine approval color my tone. "Better than I expected, honestly."

I let my hand hover there above the reddened skin of her ass for a long, suspended moment. Let her feel the radiant heat of my palm lingering just millimeters away from contact. The anticipation alone makes her tremble beneath me.

Then slowly—so slowly she could stop me if she wanted—I slide my hand lower. Down between her legs where she's been silently begging for attention since the first strike landed.

Her hips buck up immediately, instinctive and desperate. Chasing any friction I might offer. Looking for more contact, more pressure, anything to ease the unbearable ache I've built inside her.

I don't give it to her.

Instead I spread her open with both hands. Gently pull her cheeks apart so I can see everything. Her pussy gleaming wet in the late afternoon light filtering through the trees. Her tight little asshole clenching reflexively under my scrutiny. Both holes on display, vulnerable, and exposed, and mine.

My cock throbs so hard against my zipper it borders on actual pain.

Christ. She's soaked. Absolutely dripping. The evidence of her arousal has literally run down her inner thighs, leaving glistening trails on her skin.

All from my hand. From being spanked, and denied, and put exactly where I want her.

She makes this desperate, broken sound as I lean down and put my mouth on her. Half sob, half moan. The kind of noise that goes straight to my dick and makes my balls tighten.

My tongue slides between her folds and into a sweet, slick pool of her arousal. It flows onto my tongue, floods my mouth with her taste—salt and musk and something uniquely, addictively *her*.

Fuck.

She tastes even better than I imagined.

"Master," she gasps.

I force myself to pull back. I want to tell her that this is far more demanding of me than it is her—because I want to fuck every hole she has right now. Right here. Sixty feet up in the air.

But I'm never going to tell her that. Not during a game. I need her to be afraid. I need her to think I'm indifferent. And I need her to do everything I tell her anyway. So I simply say, "No."

I stand and begin unfastening her ankle cuff.

"Wait—what are you—are you letting me go?"

The hope and terror mixing in her voice is perfect.

I release her wrist next.

She stays bent over the beam for a moment, like she doesn't trust that she's actually free to move. Then she slowly turns her body to face me. Her eyes are huge. Wet. Pupils blown wide with arousal and confusion. "I don't understand."

"Station One is complete. It's time to move to Station Two."

I pull her upright, steadying her when she wobbles.

She's making these soft, desperate sounds in the back of her throat. Little whimpers that tell me exactly how badly she needs relief. How close to breaking she is.

An addict looking for her fix.

Perfect.

I turn her body toward the plank she crossed earlier. The narrow strip of ironwood extending six feet across empty air to the adjacent tree.

"Walk."

Her eyes drop immediately. Down through the gaps in the platform. Down past sixty feet of nothing to the jungle floor far below.

Her breathing changes. Shallow. Rapid.

"I can't—"

"You already did." I grip her shoulders. Firm enough to anchor her. Not gentle. "You crossed it to get the cuffs. You'll do it again to leave."

"That was different, I was crawling!"

I pet her hair, smoothing it back. Her face is glistening

with sweat, her skin flushed pink with desire. If she only knew how much I wanted to fuck her right now.

"I'm asking you to walk six feet, my pretty little slut. You don't need to crawl."

She swallows hard. Looks down. Looks back up at me with pleading eyes. "Can't we just climb down the way I came up?"

"No."

My fingers dig into her skin. She's trembling under my hands now. The arousal-driven tremors mixing with genuine fear.

This part is real risk. I'm not going to let her fall. My hands are right here. I can catch her before she goes over the edge.

But if she does fall somehow—if she panics and jerks away from me, if her foot slips on a patch of moisture, if the wood gives under her weight—there's a net strung fifteen feet below. Heavy-duty cargo netting anchored to the surrounding trees.

It will catch her.

But the canopy is thick between here and there. Branches, vines, dense foliage she'll slam through on the way down. The net will stop her from dying. It won't stop her from getting hurt.

Bruises. Scrapes. Possibly worse.

She doesn't know about the net. She thinks it's sixty feet of empty air to the ground.

"Master, please—"

"Look at me."

She drags her eyes up from the drop, looking over her shoulder until her eyes lock onto mine. Her pupils are still wide, but now tears are gathering at the corners. Her beautiful plump lips are parted and trembling.

Christ, she's beautiful when she's terrified.

"You're going to walk across that plank," I tell her. Flat.

Matter of fact. "You're going to do it now. And you're not going to fall."

"How do you know I won't—"

"Because I'm right here." I shift my grip. One hand on each shoulder. "And I'm not going to let you."

Her breath hitches.

She wants to believe me. I can see it in her eyes. The desperate need to trust that I'll keep her safe even while I'm deliberately scaring her.

"What if I can't—what if I freeze—"

"Then I'll carry you."

The words come out harsher than I intended. Edged with the frustration of wanting to just throw her over my shoulder and be done with it.

But that's not the point of this station.

She needs to walk it herself. Needs to feel the fear and do it anyway because I told her to.

That's the surrender I'm after.

"You need to trust me, Scarletta. You need to give in to me. It's my job to protect you. If you don't believe that, why are you here?"

I don't push her.

I just stand here with my hands on her shoulders and wait for her brain to catch up to what her body already knows.

She's going to do it. She's going to walk across that plank because I told her to. Because somewhere underneath all the fear and resistance, she wants to prove she can.

Wants to earn what I refused to give her five minutes ago.

Her eyes search mine. Looking for something. Permission, maybe. Or reassurance that I'm not lying about keeping her safe.

I give her nothing except steady eye contact and silence.

The waiting is its own kind of torture. For both of us.

My cock is still hard enough to pound nails. Still throbbing against my zipper from tasting her pussy and watching her come apart under my hands.

From seeing her bent over that beam with her ass red from my palm—dripping wet and desperate.

From knowing she's standing here completely naked sixty feet in the air with absolutely nowhere to hide.

The afternoon sun cuts through the canopy at an angle that hits her body perfectly. Lights up her skin in gold. Makes her look like something out of a Renaissance painting—all soft curves, and pale flesh, and classical proportions.

Except Renaissance women weren't shaved bare and trembling with denied orgasms.

Her breasts are perfect. Small enough to fit in my hands, large enough to bounce when she walks. The kind of tits that don't need a bra but look incredible in one anyway. High and firm with just enough softness that I know they'd feel like heaven pressed against my chest.

Her nipples are standing straight out. Hard little peaks that jut forward from her profile like they're begging to be touched, and pinched, and sucked.

I want to put my mouth on them. Roll them between my teeth until she gasps. Bite down just hard enough to make her cry out and clench around nothing.

I don't move.

She's still thinking. Still processing. I can see it happening behind her eyes—the war between terror and submission, between self-preservation and the desperate need to please me.

Her breathing has changed again. Deeper now. More controlled.

She's trying to calm herself down. Trying to find her courage in the middle of the panic. Her gaze drops briefly to the plank, then back to my face. Her tongue darts out to wet her lips. "You promise you won't let me fall?"

The question comes out small. Vulnerable. Nothing like

the confident, filthy writer who pens stories about women being chased through forests and fucked against trees.

This is the real Scarletta underneath all those fantasies.

Scared. Uncertain. Desperate for someone to tell her she's safe even while putting her in danger.

"I promise."

Two words. Absolute. No elaboration needed.

Her chest rises and falls with another deep breath. Her nipples tighten even further with the movement, if that's even physically possible.

Christ.

I want to fuck her so badly right now that my hands are shaking with the effort of staying still.

But this moment isn't about what I want. It's about what she needs to give me.

Trust. Surrender. Obedience even when every instinct screams at her to refuse.

She swallows hard. Then... she begins to cry. "I trusted another man before."

"I know," I say, brushing the back of my knuckles against her cheek. She leans into my touch like a wounded baby seeking comfort.

"He..." she sucks in a deep, trembling breath. "He..." She looks over her shoulder at me. Her eyes find mine. They are gushing tears. "He... raped me."

It occurs to me that she's never admitted that before. Not to herself. That maybe she took the blame. She didn't signal enough. She didn't stop him in time. She let it go too far.

"I know that too," I say, placing both my hands on her face. "I killed him for that, Scarletta. Tortured him. Made him pay."

She nods, eyes drifting away now as her chin trembles. "If I trust you and..."

She doesn't finish. But I already know what she's going to say. "If you trust me and I let you down, you'll never trust anyone again."

She nods, more tears. Some hiccuping sobs. They ride down her cheeks, soaking into my hands that are still holding her face.

I shift my grip to her shoulders and turn her slowly toward me. Both hands cupping her jaw now. My thumbs brush away the tears still streaming down her cheeks.

The platform isn't designed for two people standing this close. We're sixty feet up and I'm repositioning her weight while she's crying and vulnerable and not thinking clearly about where her feet are.

If she panics, if she jerks away from me, if I miscalculate the angle—we both go over.

The net will catch us. Probably. If we don't get tangled in vines first or slam into a branch hard enough to crack ribs.

I do it anyway.

I need her looking at me when I fix this.

Her eyes are red-rimmed and swollen. Her lips are trembling.

Beautiful.

I lean down and kiss her.

Soft. Controlled. Nothing like the rough claiming I've been doing to her body for the past hour.

Just my mouth on hers. Gentle pressure. My lips moving against hers with deliberate tenderness.

She makes this shocked little sound against my lips. Like she can't process that I'm capable of kissing her like this after everything else.

Her lips are warm. Soft. They taste like salt.

I like it.

Not as much as having my fingers buried in her pussy while she begs. Not as much as watching it clench around nothing while she's denied release.

But I like it more than I expected to.

I pull back just enough to look at her face. Her eyes are

still wet but they're focused on me now instead of spiraling inward with fear.

Good.

"You're my good little slut," I tell her. Quiet. Steady. "And you're going to walk across that plank because I'm asking you to."

She shakes her head, crying harder now.

"Scarletta," I say, my voice softer than I ever thought it could be. "Come on. You're not gonna let six feet stop this day, are you? You're not gonna let six fucking feet keep you from experiencing my amazing cock again, are you?"

She snickers. Looks up. Meets my eyes.

I brush my thumbs across her cheekbones, wiping away the fresh tears that keep falling. Her eyes are locked on mine now, searching for something she doesn't know how to name.

"You've written this scene five times," I tell her. The words come out quieter than I intended. "At least."

Her brow furrows. Confusion cutting through the fear.

I should stop talking. Should turn her around and make her walk the plank and get this station over with. But my mouth keeps moving anyway.

"In *Breaking Point*, Natasha had to cross a ravine on a fallen log while her kidnapper watched from the opposite side. You wrote: 'I picture the fall. Picture my body broken on the rocks below, but his voice keeps pulling me forward—not commanding, just certain I would not fail him. Certain that I could do it.'"

Scarletta's eyes widen. Her lips part.

I'm not finished.

"In *The Ledge*, Kira had to climb up a fire escape to prove she trusted Leo. You wrote: 'Fear is trying to convince me I'm going to die, but his hands on my hips tell a different story— one where I'm already safe.'"

Her breathing has changed. Shallower now. Not from panic anymore.

"In *Running from the Rangers*, Simone jumped off a bridge holding hands with Justin because he told her the river would save them. You wrote: 'The terror is real, but so is the certainty in his eyes. He'd never let me break.'"

I watch her face as recognition floods through her. She knows these stories. Obviously. She wrote every word.

But hearing me recite them back to her—exact sentences she typed months or years ago in the safety of her apartment —that's different.

That's proof I've consumed every single thing she's ever created.

"In *Trust Fall*, Elena had to stand on the edge of a rooftop while blindfolded and wait for him to tell her when to step back. You wrote: 'I can'tsee the drop, but I can feel it pulling at me like gravity has intentions. His voice is the only thing tethering me to solid ground.'"

My thumbs are still moving across her cheeks. Wiping away tears that have slowed to a trickle now.

Her mouth opens like she wants to say something, but nothing comes out.

"And in *Depths of Despair*, Claire had to walk a makeshift bridge between two buildings to escape her captors while her master encouraged from below. You wrote: 'Every step feels like dying, but I take them anyway because losing him is worse than losing my own life.'"

I stop talking.

The silence between us feels heavier than it should. Like I've revealed something I didn't plan to give her.

Scarletta stares at me. Her eyes are still wet but they're not crying anymore. Just wide and stunned and searching my face for an explanation I'm not sure how to provide.

"You remember all of that?" Her voice comes out hoarse. Barely above a whisper.

"I remember everything you've ever written."

The truth of that statement hits me as I say it out loud. Not just the dark romance scenes I've used to plan our encounters. Not just the sex, or the bondage, or the psychological games.

All of it.

The throwaway lines about her characters drinking coffee black because they can't afford cream. The descriptions of empty apartments that smell like loneliness. The protagonists who apologize too much, and think too hard, and sabotage their own happiness.

Every word she's put on a page, I've absorbed like it was scripture.

Because it wasn't just research.

It was *her*.

The realization makes my chest tighten in a way that feels uncomfortable. Foreign. Like something shifted that wasn't supposed to move.

"Why?" she asks.

I don't have a good answer. Or maybe I do, but admitting it feels like handing her a weapon I'm not sure she knows how to use yet.

My obsession isn't just about sex. It's not even about control, though that's part of it.

It's about her talent. Her mind. The way she builds worlds, and characters, and psychological depth that most published authors can't touch. The way she understands power dynamics, and fear, and desire better than people who've spent decades studying it.

She's brilliant.

And she has no idea.

"Because you're exceptional," I tell her. The words feel too honest. Too raw. I force my voice back to something neutral. Controlled. "And exceptional things deserve to be appreciated."

Her eyes search mine. Looking for the lie. The manipulation.

She won't find it.

This is the truth, even if I'm wrapping it in language that sounds like dominance instead of devotion.

Her laugh is belated, but real. "I write... smut, Master. It's... OK, I guess but..."

"I'm not talking about the smut." I brush my thumb across her cheekbone. "I'm talking about the way you build psychological tension. The way you understand character motivation. You could write beautiful literary fiction if you wanted to. Dark literary fiction that would make critics uncomfortable and readers obsessed."

She stares at me like I just told her she could fly.

"No one's ever—" Her voice cracks. "No one's ever said that to me. In person, I mean. It's... thank you."

The confession breaks something in my chest I didn't know was locked.

She's twenty-two years old. She's been writing since she was a teenager. Posting stories online for years. Pouring her talent, and darkness, and brilliance into thousands of words that strangers consume and comment on.

And no one has ever looked her in the eye and told her she's good at it.

Not her mother. Not her professors before she dropped out. Not the ex-boyfriend I killed for raping her.

No one.

Until me.

She reaches up and touches my face. Her fingertips trace along my jaw. My cheekbone. The corner of my mouth.

"You're really hot," she whispers.

I laugh.

I actually laugh.

Not the controlled chuckle I use to put people at ease or the dark amusement I feel when I'm hunting. A real laugh that catches me off guard with how genuine it feels.

"That's what you're thinking about right now?"

"You took off the mask." Her fingers keep exploring my

face like she's memorizing it. "I thought you'd be... I don't know. Scarier looking. But you're just really attractive and it's confusing."

I kiss her again. Harder this time. My tongue sliding between her lips to taste her properly. She opens for me immediately, letting me in, kissing me back with desperate enthusiasm that makes my cock throb.

When I pull away, we're both breathing hard.

"Backwards," I murmur against her mouth. "Small steps. I've got you."

I walk her. Slow. Controlled. My hands on her waist now, guiding her.

She's gasping into my mouth as I kiss her between each step. Her pulse hammering so hard I can feel it vibrating through her skin.

"That's it. Good girl."

Her heel finds the edge of the plank. Six feet of narrow wood between her and the adjacent tree. Nothing but air on either side. She whimpers.

"Eyes on me," I tell her. "Not down. Just me."

Another step back. Her foot settles on the wood. It doesn't wobble. Doesn't creak. Solid and stable under her weight just like I promised.

"I've got you."

I keep kissing her. Keep my hands firm on her waist. Keep walking her backwards inch by inch while her breathing comes in sharp, terrified gasps against my lips.

Her back foot finds the platform on the other side.

She made it.

CHAPTER 6
SCARLETTA

I can't stop replaying it.

The masked man's mouth on mine. The way he kissed me between steps while I was terrified of falling. The way his hands felt on my waist, steadying me.

You're exceptional.

No one's ever said that to me. Not in person. Not looking at my face while they said it.

Online, sure. Anonymous praise from faceless usernames. But that's different. That's not real. That's people reacting to words on a screen, not to me.

He called my writing brilliant. Said I could do literary fiction. Dark literary fiction that would make critics uncomfortable.

I want to believe him.

God, I want to believe him so badly it hurts.

And his face. Jesus Christ, his face.

I wasn't expecting that either. I thought the mask was hiding something. Scars maybe. Or average features. Something that would make the mystery make sense.

But he's just... handsome. Actually handsome. Sharp

jawline, intense eyes, the kind of bone structure that makes you want to keep looking.

It makes me want to please him more. Makes me want to earn his approval. Makes the ache between my thighs even worse because now I can picture his face while I imagine all the things he might do to me.

Pathetic. I'm so fucking pathetic.

But I don't care.

I step fully onto the platform and realize how narrow it is. Just a ring of wood surrounding the massive tree trunk. Barely wide enough for one person to stand on, definitely not wide enough for two.

I turn around to ask him what I'm supposed to do now… and find him walking back across the plank. Away from me. Heading toward the opposite tree where the rope ladder waits.

"Wait—where are you going?"

He glances back over his shoulder with this devastating smile. The kind that promises trouble. "This isn't a pre-school, my good little slut. It's a master class. You don't get your hand held twice. You want my cock, little whore? You gotta earn it."

His words land like a slap.

"You've already taken more from me than you've earned. You're in debt, my horny little trollop. So my last bit of advice to you—" He reaches down between his legs and grabs himself. "—if you want this big, hard cock inside your dripping wet pussy— is to exceed my expectations. Otherwise…" he shrugs. "I'll edge you forever. Deny you forever. Leave you alone… *forever*."

Before I can pick my fucking jaw back up off the ground, he reaches up into the canopy and pulls something. A handle. Hidden in the leaves.

Then he jumps.

"What the—"

He disappears on a zip line that materializes from

nowhere, his body swinging down through the trees with perfect control.

Gone.

Just... gone.

I stare at the empty space where he was standing three seconds ago.

"Are you fucking kidding me?" I yell into the jungle.

No answer.

Of course no answer.

And that threat? What the fuck? Did we not just have a moment? Because to me, it felt like a moment. He kissed me, talked sweet to me, helped me.

And he abandoned you, Scarletta. Just like all the rest.

I press my back against the tree trunk and try to breathe. What is happening.

It's a challenge, obviously. I didn't fail the first one, the punishment—which was good, and hard, and still stings but in the most delicious way—was a set up from the preparation room.

I was meant to fail.

But this is different.

He doesn't want me to fail this challenge because if he did, he would've left me up here before walking the plank, not after helping me across.

Which means…

Still pressing my back against the tree, I lean over a little, trying to see the other side of the tree.

Sure enough, there's a platform. And nailed to the platform is an envelope.

Challenge two.

I need to move. It's literally like eighteen inches to the other side of the tree, but it's a really long way down. I look. I can't help it. I think I see a net. In fact, I'm pretty sure I do see a net, which makes sense because this place seems to be set up like a corporate retreat challenge exercise. If those came with naked women and gyno-tubs.

This is a professional set up. A real place that does business. Probably not corporate team-building, but something for billionaires. Like the auction.

Fake enough to keep you from dying, real enough to scare the fuck out of you.

The point of the hunt—which doesn't quite fit so far. He's not hunting me, so I don't get it. But anyway, the point of this is to trust him. He made that perfectly clear. He got me across the plank. Now I need to step up and show him that I *do* trust him. That every single thing he asks me to do here is *safe*.

Because he set it up, because he's watching.

It's a good story. Slightly twisted. Maybe too twisted for my readers. They like a good subplot, but only if it's attached to spice.

And this subplot certainly is.

God, the way he licked me.

Last time I missed most of that. I get that it happened—intellectually, I know his mouth was on me, his tongue working me over—but I don't *remember* feeling it. Not really. The whole experience exists in fragments, disjointed snapshots that don't quite connect into a coherent memory.

This time, though... this time I definitely felt it. Every single second of it.

I bet he puts his whole mouth across my pussy. Not just his tongue—his entire mouth. Seals it over me and *sucks*, pulling at my clit while his tongue flicks and presses and explores.

And that beard stubble of his... holy shit. I can still feel the ghost of it scratching the inside of my thighs, rubbing them raw in the best possible way. The slight burn mixing with the wet heat of his mouth, the contrast making everything sharper, more intense.

I let out a long, shaky breath, my pussy throbbing hard

just picturing his mouth between my legs again. His grey eyes looking up at me while he devours me, watching my face while he tears me apart with that skilled, relentless tongue.

"All right, Scarletta," I mutter to myself, trying to shake off the heat building between my legs. "If you want his big, hard cock in your sopping wet pussy again—exceed his expectations."

I snicker at my own ridiculous internal pep talk.

But yeah. I'll do it.

Whatever it takes.

I inch my way around the tree trunk, keeping my back pressed against the rough bark. The platform is exactly what I thought it would be—a small wooden ledge that feels stable enough under my bare feet.

I exhale hard, my heart still racing, but slowing down now that I'm not actively terrified of plummeting to my death.

"See? You did it," I whisper to myself.

And I actually did. Without him holding my hand this time. Without his mouth distracting me or his voice guiding me.

I kind of want him to acknowledge that. To tell me I did good.

But he's not here, so I bend down and pick up the envelope that's nailed to the platform.

The paper feels expensive between my fingers. Heavy card stock, the kind you'd use for wedding invitations. I break the wax seal—because of course there's a wax seal—and pull out the card.

My filthy little Valentine wants to earn my cock,

Square your shoulders, set your jaw, and prepare yourself for shock.

Zip down the line to station 2, trust gravity and steel—

At the end you'll get your chance to be fucked with something real.

Spread wide upon the cross you'll wait, exposed for all to see,

Then maybe if you're very good, I'll let you come for me.

I read it twice.

Then a third time because my brain is struggling to process the words "exposed for all to see."

Who's *all*? Who the fuck is watching this besides him?

I glance up at the harness suspended from the zip line. It's professional grade—thick nylon straps, metal carabiners, the kind of equipment rock climbers use. Not some sketchy DIY project that's going to snap halfway through.

He wouldn't let me fall. I know that now.

The plank proved it. He walked me across. Kissed me between steps. Made it feel like the most natural thing in the world to trust him sixty feet in the air.

And the way he touched my face after. Gentle. Almost reverent.

That wasn't part of the plan. I don't think it was, anyway. The kiss felt spontaneous. Like he wanted to do it and just... did.

Like maybe he actually likes me.

Not just my body, or my stories, or the way I submit to him. But *me*.

Which is insane. I know it's insane. He's a literal murderer who's been stalking me for six months and orchestrated an entire fake auction just to own me.

But he also killed Derek. For me. Because Derek hurt me.

And he memorized my stories. Not just read them—*memorized* them. Quoted them back to me word for word.

He thinks I'm exceptional.

I look at the harness again, studying how it's designed. Two leg loops, a waist belt, and a chest strap. The attachment point connects to a pulley system on the zip line cable.

This is just like the corporate team-building courses I've seen in movies. Except those people wear clothes and don't have "spread wide upon the cross" waiting for them at the end.

My pussy clenches at the thought.

A cross. He's going to strap me to a cross and fuck me.

And people will see.

The cameras. Of course there are cameras. There were cameras at the auction, cameras in my apartment, cameras everywhere he wants them.

He gets off on watching me. On knowing other people are watching me too.

I should be horrified.

Instead, I'm so wet I can feel it on my inner thighs.

"This is fucked up, Scarletta," I mutter, but my hands are already reaching for the harness.

I step into the leg loops first, pulling them up around my thighs. The nylon feels secure against my bare skin. I fasten the waist belt, checking that it's snug but not cutting off circulation. Then I clip the chest strap and double-check every connection point.

My fingers are shaking but not from fear this time.

From anticipation.

He wants me to trust gravity and steel. To let go and fly down this line into whatever's waiting for me at Station Two.

And I'm going to do it.

Not because I'm brave—I'm definitely not brave—but because he's watching. Because he's waiting for me. Because every single thing I do here is proof that I trust him.

And maybe he'll reward me for it.

Maybe he'll finally let me come.

I walk to the edge of the platform, the harness clips jangling with each step. The zip line stretches out through the canopy, disappearing into the jungle below. I can't see where it ends.

I grab the overhead cable with both hands, feeling the solid steel beneath my palms.

My heart pounds so hard I can hear it in my ears.

"Okay," I whisper. "Exceed his expectations."

Then I jump.

The world drops away and I'm flying.

Actually flying. Wind rushing past my naked body, my hair whipping behind me, the cable singing above my head as the pulley races down the line.

A bird explodes out of the canopy right in front of me and I scream, half terror and half laughter, because what the hell else can I do? My feet dangle beneath me, completely useless, and the harness digs into my thighs in a way that's almost sexual, the pressure right where my legs meet my body.

I crash through a spider web and feel the sticky threads catch across my face and chest. I'm laughing now, really laughing, wiping frantically at my skin because, Jesus Christ there better not be a spider on me, but I can't stop grinning like an idiot.

This is insane.

This is completely fucking insane and I'm doing it.

Me. Scarletta Desmond, who hasn't left her apartment for anything except groceries and eviction notices in two years. Who ate Lucky Charms for dinner standing at her kitchen counter because sitting at a table felt too much like admitting she was alone.

I tilt my head back and look up at the canopy rushing past above me. Sunlight filters through the leaves in scattered patches, dappled gold and green, the kind of light photographers chase and I've only ever seen in screensavers.

It's beautiful.

God, it's so beautiful I could cry.

A lizard skitters across a branch as I zoom past, its tail flicking in annoyance at being disturbed. More birds scatter, their squawks echoing through the trees like they're gossiping about the naked girl flying through their neighborhood.

I wonder if this is what freedom feels like. Not the idea of freedom I write about in my stories where my heroines are free because they've surrendered to someone stronger. But actual freedom. The kind where you're moving through space with nothing holding you back except physics and good engineering.

Except I'm not free, am I? I'm strapped into a harness, following instructions on a card, performing for cameras I can't see and a man who's probably watching every second of this.

And I don't care.

I actually don't care because this feels too good to ruin with overthinking.

The cable starts to angle differently and I realize I'm slowing down. The trees thin out slightly, opening into a clearing I can see approaching. My speed drops from exhilarating, to manageable, to gentle, and then I'm gliding the last few feet like I've done this a thousand times before.

My feet touch ground and I stumble slightly, catching myself with a hand on the cable above me.

Perfect landing.

I did it. I actually did it, and I didn't die, and it was *incredible*.

I'm breathing hard, my chest heaving, and I can feel the adrenaline coursing through my entire body. My hands shake as I start unclipping the harness, fumbling with the carabiners because my fingers won't cooperate.

Then I hear it.

Voices. Soft. Distant. Maybe twenty feet away?

I freeze with one leg still in the harness, listening.

"...stunning, isn't she?"

Male voice. Cultured accent, maybe British?

"Absolutely exquisite." Different voice, also male. American, deeper.

My heart stops beating for a full second.

People. There are people here. Watching me.

I yank my leg free from the harness and spin around, scanning the trees, but I can't see anyone. The jungle is too thick, too layered with ferns, and vines, and shadows.

But they're there.

They can see me and I can't see them, and they just called me stunning.

My pussy clenches so hard I gasp.

Oh God.

Oh God, this is actually happening. This is real. There are strangers watching me right now, looking at my naked body, and they think I'm exquisite.

Heat floods through me, starting low in my belly and spreading outward until my skin feels like it's burning. My nipples are so hard they ache and the wetness between my legs intensifies to the point where I can feel it starting to slide down my inner thighs.

I should be mortified. I should be covering myself, hiding, demanding to know who they are and what they're doing here.

Instead I'm standing here with my thighs pressed together, trying desperately not to touch myself because I'm so close to coming I might actually do it without any stimulation at all.

This is what I wrote about. All those stories where my heroines are displayed, examined, watched by men they can't see. Where their bodies are evaluated and discussed like they're objects on display.

I'm living it right now.

And it's so much more intense than I ever imagined it would be.

Another voice murmurs something I can't quite hear and someone laughs softly.

They're talking about me. Commenting on me. Probably noting every detail of my body, every imperfection I've spent years hiding under baggy clothes and blanket forts.

My breathing comes faster, shallower. My clit throbs with every heartbeat.

I need to move. I need to follow the instructions, do whatever comes next, or I'm going to stand here and come in front of these invisible strangers just from knowing they're watching.

The cross.

He said there'd be a cross at Station Two.

I force my legs to work and take a shaky step forward. Then another. My whole body feels hypersensitive, like every nerve ending is firing at once. The air moving across my skin feels obscene. The way my thighs brush together with each step sends sparks straight to my pussy.

And then I see it.

A large wooden cross mounted vertically in a cleared area about fifteen feet ahead. Dark wood, smooth and polished, with leather restraints attached at four points. Wrist height. Ankle height.

Spread wide upon the cross you'll wait, exposed for all to see.

Jesus Christ, he meant it literally.

A small white card rests on the ground at the base of the cross, propped against the wood.

I walk toward it on legs that barely support my weight, feeling eyes tracking my every movement. Wondering if they can see how wet I am. If they can tell from the way I'm walking that I'm desperate, aching, ready to break.

I pick up the card with shaking fingers.

Whatever it says, I'll do it.

All of it.

Every single thing.

Because I'm in.

I'm completely, irrevocably in, and there's no part of me that wants to be anywhere else.

CHAPTER 7
CALEB

The door to the hidden control room between stations 1 and 2 blends in to vegetation-covered rock wall. Primitive and natural. But inside, it's climate-controlled space dominated by a wall of monitors that hum with low electric frequency that makes the air feel charged.

On one side of the wall the screens show Dimitri Volkov's pathetic progress through the mud on Chaff Island. He got hit with the honey about an hour back and he's been desperately trying to wash it off as the bugs begin to eat him alive.

He is irrelevant right now, so I turn my attention to the other side of the wall of screens, take a seat, and begin switching camera angels around until I find her.

Scarletta stands exactly where I left her on the high platform. It's only been about three minutes, so her hesitation doesn't mean much.

Yet.

I watch her face closely as the reality of my abandonment sinks in.

What will she do?

Give up?

If I thought she would give up at Station 1, I'd never have wasted my time bringing her here.

She's not going to give up.

The question is, how long does she need to fight back the shame?

That's what's really going on inside Scarletta's head. Her own voice is her prison. Her own thoughts, her own mind, *herself*.

It's not about Derek.

It's never been about Derek.

Scarletta wants to know why she's so fucked up. Why she keeps attracting men who want to disrespect her, hurt her, leave her.

But she's learning quickly. Giving in to her attendants the way she did. There was no pretending this time. No story being concocted in her head about what this *is* and what this *isn't*.

It's not a look on her face that marks the shift here. She doesn't do some theatrical gritting of her teeth or hardening of her jaw.

She simply... lets out a breath. A very small breath. And with it, her shoulders drop. Not in defeat, but in resolve.

She isn't thinking about her past right now.

She's thinking about *me*.

She's thinking about earning the right to have my cock inside her. The right to be granted permission to come. The right to scream, and sob, and shatter completely under the expert, unrelenting hands of a true master who knows exactly how to unmake her.

It's fucking beautiful.

She moves toward the hanging harness. Her hands shake as she steps into the leather straps with a clumsy urgency that makes my cock twitch hard against my zipper.

She wants to chase me.

The camera angle is merciless. It captures everything. As

she bends to secure the leg loops, the sunlight filters through the leaves and illuminates the gleaming, swollen flesh between her thighs. She is impossibly wet.

Her pussy is puffy and pink, leaking her desire. It coats her inner legs and glistens in the high-definition feed. A biological testament to how thoroughly I have already rewired her.

She is terrified of falling sixty feet to the jungle floor, yet her body is already underneath me. Already in the middle of being fucked.

She tightens the metal buckle across her hips. The thick nylon digs into her soft skin, pressing directly against the desperate ache I left unresolved. She pauses for a second, looking out at the expanse of green nothingness before her.

There is no grimace of terror on her face now. Her lips are parted, panting slightly. Her pupils are wide and alert. This is pure, unadulterated excitement.

Sometimes the challenges make women wilt. They uncover cowards. Not everyone is a main character, after all.

But Scarletta doesn't fancy herself an NPC.

In every story, she's *the woman*. The one who matters. The one who craves things. Who has burning desires that lead to risks, which lead to rewards.

This is *her* story.

She jumps.

The cable sings under her weight. Friction and physics and velocity conspiring to send her rocketing through the jungle canopy at a speed I calculated precisely to terrify without causing actual harm.

I lean closer to the screen, tracking her descent through three different camera angles simultaneously. Her face is a study in contradictions. Terror and elation fight for dominance across her features as she careens toward Station 2.

She doesn't scream. I expected screaming. Most women

scream on the zip line, even the ones who claim they love adrenaline.

Scarletta just breathes hard through her nose, eyes wide and locked on the approaching platform like she's afraid if she blinks, she'll lose her nerve entirely.

When her feet touch down on the landing zone, she stumbles forward two steps before catching herself against the wooden railing. Her chest heaves. Her legs shake.

But she's smiling.

That small, private smile she thinks no one sees when she finishes writing a chapter that surprises even herself. The one that says she's just discovered something new about who she actually is underneath all the shame and self-loathing.

I smile with her. I can't help it. This woman has no idea how fucking magnificent she looks right now.

She's fumbling with the harness buckles, still trembling from the adrenaline spike, when I activate the speakers.

Male voices filter through the hidden audio system.

"Look at her. Absolutely stunning."

"God, she's exquisite. Look at that body."

"Is she trembling? I think she's trembling."

"Of course she's trembling. Wouldn't you be?"

Scarletta freezes. Her eyes wide, mouth slightly open, breathing shallow. I can almost hear her thoughts.

Men. Watching me.

Her thighs press together, almost involuntarily, and then she snaps out of it and extracts herself from the final loop of harness.

The voices continue their casual assessment of her naked flesh, commenting on her curves, her skin, the visible evidence of her arousal.

Her nipples harden further. She wants to be seen. Almost all her stories have some voyeurism in them. The women are typically the exhibitionists, the men, voyeurs.

I am not interested in sharing Scarletta with anyone. Not

even for watching. Not even with men who are paying obscene amounts of money for the privilege.

But the attendants are different. They're professionals executing a job with clear boundaries and explicit instructions. There's no personal investment, no possessive intent, and therefore, no threat.

Random clients are an entirely different category of risk.

The men who come to Story Island are exactly like me. Sick, sadistic fucks who get off on violence and control. They pay me extraordinary sums to indulge their darkest urges in a place where evidence disappears and witnesses never existed.

Most of them have never even tried to separate the control from the violence the way I do. They don't understand the difference between dominance and cruelty, between pushing boundaries and obliterating them entirely.

They want to hurt women.

Ask me how I know…

Should any of my clients cross a line without permission… well, I become invested. I do a very thorough background check on every man who enters my establishments. I know *everything* about them.

Are they sadistic pieces of shit?

Evil, sick, insane?

Yes. Yes, yes, and yes.

I don't want to hurt women. I simply want to own one.

This is not the same thing.

But if I turned down every sadistic, evil, sick, insane piece of shit who filled out my application, my business would not exist.

Even a powerful man like Volk has to follow the rules. Because once he tips those scales, they *must* be balanced.

That's why one side of my wall of screens shows Scarletta discovering what it feels like to be an object of desire. The other side shows Volk discovering what it feels like to be prey.

One of them is coming home with me.

The other is already dead, he just doesn't know it yet.

Scarletta approaches the cross with the kind of reverent hesitation that tells me everything I need to know about what's happening inside her head.

She's not afraid of the cross.

She's afraid of how much she wants it.

The St. Andrew's Cross stands between two mahogany trees, powder-coated black steel bolted directly into living wood. Eight feet tall. Magnetic restraint points positioned at wrists, ankles, waist, and throat. The moss beneath it is soft and green, carefully maintained to cushion kneeling or collapse. Ferns have been cleared in a fifteen-foot radius to ensure unobstructed camera angles from every direction.

I designed this station myself. Every bolt. Every angle. Every sight line.

Scarletta bends to retrieve the laminated instruction card from its wooden holder at the base of the cross. The movement exposes the glistening cleft between her thighs, and I watch the camera feed capture the evidence of her arousal in merciless high definition.

She reads the card.

I know exactly what it says because I wrote it.

Simple instructions. Clear parameters. No ambiguity.

My attention shifts to the biometric panel on my left. Scarletta's vitals scroll across the screen in real-time, transmitted from the fitness tracker app loaded on her wrist.

Calling it a watch would be like calling the desert a sand box. It's a medical-grade monitoring device that tracks her heart rate, blood oxygen, skin conductance, and core body temperature with surgical precision.

Her heart is fluttering like a a bird's.

But this isn't fear. She's not afraid, she's excited.

The distinction matters. Fear produces cortisol spikes that show up in skin conductance readings as erratic fluctuations.

What I'm seeing on Scarletta's biometric feed is sustained elevation with steady conductance. That's anticipation. That's desire building toward a peak she knows is coming.

Her body is already preparing itself for what I'm about to do to her.

I reach for the audio control panel and slide the volume dial three notches higher. The recorded voices fill the clearing around Station 2 with increased presence.

"God, look at her standing there."

"She knows we're watching. Look how she's holding that card."

"I'd pay double for that one."

"Triple. Did you see her file? The things she writes..."

Scarletta's head turns slightly, scanning the tree line. Her heart rate ticks up to one hundred and twenty-two. She can't locate the source of the voices, can't determine how many men are observing her or from what distance.

That uncertainty is intentional.

I key the signal to the attendants. Three short pulses on the encrypted frequency they're monitoring.

Movement in the trees behind Scarletta. She's facing the cross, back exposed, exactly as the instruction card directed. The positioning makes it nearly impossible for her to see the three figures emerging from the carefully concealed access path.

They're dressed immaculately. Black tuxedos with satin lapels. White gloves. Venetian masks in matte black that obscure their features while maintaining a theatrical elegance that fits the fantasy I've constructed.

Scarletta doesn't know these are the same three men who bathed her, shaved her, brought her to orgasm in the stone tub. Her conscious mind would recognize them if she saw their faces, but the masks prevent that recognition. And in her current state of arousal and sensory overload, her brain is highly suggestible.

She'll accept what I want her to accept.

That's the art of what I do here. Every detail serves the narrative. The lighting. The soundscape. The costumes. The choreography. Nothing is accidental. Nothing is improvised.

Story Island exists because I understand that fantasy requires infrastructure. Most people who harbor dark desires never act on them because the logistics seem insurmountable. Where would you find a consenting partner? How would you ensure privacy? What about evidence, consequences—the mundane realities that puncture erotic imagination like needles through soap bubbles.

I eliminate those obstacles.

I build the stage, hire the players, write the script, and direct the performance. My clients pay extraordinary sums for the privilege of stepping into fantasies they couldn't construct on their own.

And the participants—the women who come here voluntarily, who sign contracts, and negotiate terms, and receive compensation that changes their lives—they get to experience what they've only imagined.

Everyone leaves satisfied.

Everyone leaves *alive*.

That's what separates my legitimate operation from the darker corners of this industry. Consent. Compensation. Careful screening. Extensive aftercare. I'm not trafficking women or exploiting vulnerability. I'm providing a service that fills a genuine need on both sides of the transaction.

The men who attend my auctions are sick fucks, certainly. But so am I. The difference is that I've channeled my sickness into something sustainable. Something that doesn't leave bodies in its wake.

Most of the time.

The first attendant reaches Scarletta and places a gloved hand on her shoulder. She startles, spine straightening, breath catching audibly on the directional microphones I've positioned throughout the clearing.

"Easy," the attendant murmurs. Of course, he's not speaking. It's a recording that comes from a small speaker on his lapel. None of the voices she will hear will be familiar.

Until she hears mine.

"You're safe," the voice tells her.

She doesn't turn around. The instruction card told her not to move, and she's following orders with a compliance that makes my cock strain painfully against my zipper.

The second attendant approaches from her left. The third from her right. Three sets of gloved hands making contact with her naked flesh simultaneously.

Her heart rate spikes to one hundred and thirty-four.

"Beautiful," one voice says.

"Responsive," another observes, trailing fingers down her spine.

"Eager," the third adds, cupping her breast with professional precision.

Scarletta moans.

The sound travels through the microphone array and fills my control room with crystalline clarity. It's not a performance moan, not the theatrical sounds women make when they think they're supposed to be enjoying themselves.

This is involuntary.

Desperate.

Pulled from somewhere deep in her chest by hands she can't see attached to men she believes are strangers.

Her biometrics confirm what I'm hearing. Heart rate elevated but steady. Skin conductance rising in the smooth curve that indicates genuine arousal rather than stress. Core temperature increasing point by point as blood flows to her extremities and her center simultaneously.

She is exactly where I want her.

The attendants guide her toward the cross with choreographed efficiency, turning her around as they gracefully maneuver to stay just out of her sightline.

She gets glimpses of them. Stuttered, jagged images that will fill her erotic dreams for years—possibly her entire life, if I'm any good at what I do.

But they are careful to perpetuate the mystery, not reveal it.

One takes her right wrist and lifts it to the corresponding restraint point. The magnetic cuff closes around her flesh with a soft click that registers on multiple microphones.

Left wrist. Click.

Right ankle. Click.

Left ankle. Click.

She's spread now. Fully exposed. Her back against the smooth steel of the cross, her front facing the jungle clearing where hidden cameras capture every trembling breath.

The waist restraint engages. Then the throat collar, adjusted loose enough to allow breathing and swallowing but tight enough to remind her constantly of its presence.

Scarletta whimpers.

The attendants step aside. Their work is done for now. They'll remain in the clearing, visible at the edges of her peripheral vision, maintaining the illusion of an audience while I make my way to claim what belongs to me.

I rise from my chair and take one final look at the left wall of monitors.

Volk has made progress. He's no longer in the mud pit where I last observed him. The cameras track his stumbling path through the undergrowth of Chaff Island, his naked body caked with honey residue and whatever organic material has adhered to it during his desperate attempts to wash himself clean.

I zoom the camera on his torso.

The image resolves into clarity, and I see exactly what I expected. A column of red ants marching up from his hip toward his chest. Fire ants. The island has an abundant population of them, attracted by the synthetic honey compound that's now embedded in every pore of Volk's skin.

Each bite delivers a small dose of venom. Individually, the stings are merely painful. Cumulatively, over hours, they produce systemic inflammation that will eventually compromise his cardiovascular system.

Volk is trying to brush them off, but his movements are sluggish. The honey is acting as an adhesive, trapping the ants against his flesh even as they sting him repeatedly. He's learning that every solution creates a new problem.

I zoom further, wanting to observe the pattern of welts developing across his ribcage.

The image blurs.

I adjust the focus.

The blur persists, flickering at the edges with digital artifacts that indicate hardware malfunction rather than simple calibration issues.

I try a different camera angle. Same result. The secondary feeds from Chaff Island are all exhibiting the same degradation, though to varying degrees. Some cameras are functional. Others are producing images that are nearly unwatchable.

Irritation tightens my jaw.

This is unacceptable.

I pull up the maintenance log and schedule a comprehensive camera review for the coming week. Every unit on Chaff Island will need to be inspected, cleaned, and potentially replaced. The salt air and humidity take a toll on electronics, even military-grade equipment rated for harsh environments.

I should have anticipated this. Should have scheduled preventive maintenance before initiating the current operation. The fact that I didn't represents a lapse in my usual standards.

Volk will suffer regardless of whether I can watch in perfect clarity. The outcome isn't affected by the quality of my surveillance. But the documentation matters. When this is over, when his body has been reduced to ash and scattered across international waters, I want to have a complete record of what he experienced.

Justice requires witness.

I make a note to have my technical team prioritize the Chaff Island array and then dismiss the irritation from my thoughts. Dwelling on imperfection serves no purpose. The situation is what it is. Volk is being eaten alive by insects while Scarletta writhes against magnetic restraints under the hands of my attendants.

One screen shows punishment.

The other shows reward.

Both are exactly where they're supposed to be.

I power down my personal console, leaving the automated systems to continue their monitoring. The control room will record everything in my absence. Multiple redundancies ensure that no moment goes uncaptured, even if I'm not present to observe in real-time.

The door to the hidden control room seals behind me with a soft hiss of pressure equalization. Outside, the jungle is alive with sound and motion. Birds calling. Insects humming. The distant crash of waves against volcanic rock.

Station 2 is a twelve-minute walk from here along the primary access trail. I could take the service path and cut that time in half, but I'm not in a hurry. Scarletta isn't going anywhere. The restraints will hold her exactly as I've configured them, exposed and waiting, her arousal building with every passing second.

Anticipation is its own form of torture.

She'll be desperate by the time I arrive. Trembling. Begging. Ready to surrender whatever final fragments of resistance she's been clutching.

I begin walking.

CHAPTER 8
SCARLETTA

The cross holds me in place like I'm a specimen pinned for examination.

I can't move my arms or legs. The restraint across my waist keeps me from arching away from the steel, and the collar around my throat forces my head into a position where I have to stare straight ahead into the jungle instead of looking down at my own exposed body.

I'm waiting.

I don't know for what, exactly. Or for whom.

I'm hoping it's him. The unmasked man who kissed me on the plank. The handsome man who called my writing exceptional and made me feel like maybe I'm not just broken garbage pretending to be functional.

But I've learned not to assume anything since the auction.

Whoever he is, the point of all this is to force me to admit that I'm not the one in control here—*he* is. That everything happening to me is *his* design. That I'm not a participant in this experience—I'm the *subject* of it.

The voices around me continue their commentary.

I think the hands that strapped me to this cross belong to the attendants from earlier., but I couldn't get a good enough look at them when they emerged from the trees to make that determination with certainty. They were masked. Dressed in black tuxedos instead of white linen.

The voices are definitely different, though. And they're amplified, like they're coming from everywhere, all at once. Ever since they put me on the cross, the've been making comments. Not *about* me. Not clinical observations delivered in neutral tones. They're saying things designed to *arouse* me. To provoke me. To stimulate responses I can't control.

One of them describes how he's going to fuck my throat until I choke when he's given permission.

Another one details exactly how he'll spread my ass and work his tongue inside me while I writhe against the cross, helpless to stop him.

The third voice—lower, rougher—tells me he's going to fist my pussy until I squirt all over his hand and then make me lick myself off his fingers.

My pussy clenches.

God. I'm so wet I can feel it running down my inner thighs.

But I'm not so far gone—not so consumed by arousal— that my critical thinking skills have completely shut down.

This is another test.

The masked man is diabolically cunning. I understand that now. Every challenge has layers. Every instruction contains traps I don't recognize until I've already fallen into them.

He set me up to fail at the bathing pavilion. Let the attendants touch me knowing I'd come without permission, knowing he could punish me for it later.

This feels similar.

These voices describing filthy acts they want to perform on my restrained body—they're trying to provoke me. To arouse me. So that when the unmasked man comes, I will fall apart immediately.

It doesn't matter who these three men are. What matters is that they're watching me. That they can see how swollen my pussy is. How hard my nipples have gone. How my body trembles against the restraints not from fear but from desperate, aching need.

I like the fact that they're watching.

I like knowing they want me.

I like hearing them describe exactly what they'd do if given permission.

And, if the unmasked man gave them permission... I would like them to do that stuff to me.

The minutes tick by.

I wait.

And wait.

And wait.

The voices continue their commentary, growing filthier with each passing moment. Describing double penetration. Describing how they'd use my holes in rotation. Describing how they'd make me service all three of them at once until I'm nothing but a wet, used mess.

My clit throbs.

My body betrays me.

The arch of my spine lifts my breasts higher, pulls the collar tighter against my windpipe until each breath requires effort. My ankles strain inward against the magnetic cuffs, muscles burning with the useless need to close my thighs and create friction. My wrists twist in their restraints, skin rubbing raw as I reach instinctively for my own pussy—knowing I can't touch, knowing it's pointless, unable to stop trying.

The ache between my legs has become unbearable.

I want them to touch me.

To fuck me. To do the things they're describing.

I'm pathetic.

I know I'm pathetic.

But I can't stop wanting it.

Movement in the jungle behind me makes me startle.

My heart slams against my ribs.

Is it him? Is the unmasked man finally here?

I can't turn my head to look. The collar holds me facing forward. I can only listen to the footsteps approaching through the undergrowth, growing louder as whoever it is gets closer.

The voices around me go silent.

Footsteps stop directly behind the cross.

Behind *me*.

I hold my breath.

Large, rough hands slide over my hips from behind, gripping my flesh with enough pressure that I feel claimed. Owned. The calluses on his palms scrape against my skin as he runs his hands up my sides, over my ribcage, then cups my breasts from behind and squeezes hard enough to make me gasp.

His body presses against my back.

I feel the heat of him through the thin layer of air between us.

His cock—thick and hard—presses against my hip through what feels like fabric. He's not naked like I am.

One hand leaves my breast and slides down my stomach. Lower. His fingers find my pussy and push inside me without hesitation. Two fingers. Maybe three. I can't tell. I'm so wet he encounters no resistance.

"Good girl," he murmurs against my ear. "You waited."

His voice.

It's him.

Relief floods through me so intensely my knees would buckle if the restraints weren't holding me upright.

My unmasked man

He's here.

His fingers curl inside me, finding that spot that makes my vision blur. His thumb finds my clit and begins circling it with exactly the right pressure. Not too hard. Not too soft.

Perfect.

Like he's memorized my body's responses.

Like he knows exactly how to make me fall apart.

"Please," I whisper.

"Please what?"

His fingers still. His thumb stops moving.

I make a desperate sound that's half sob, half moan.

"Please let me come. *Please*. I've been good. I did everything you told me to do. I crossed the plank. I took the zip line. I let them strap me here. I waited. *Please*."

The unmasked man steps around the cross and positions himself directly in front of me.

His face fills my vision. Those stunning eyes—dark, and deep, and focused with an intensity that makes my stomach flip—lock onto mine like I'm the only thing in the world worth looking at.

His jaw is sharp, covered in a shadow of stubble that I want to feel scraping against my inner thighs.

His lips are full, slightly parted, and as I watch them, they slowly curve into a smile that sends heat pooling between my legs.

God, he's beautiful.

I want to reach up and touch him. I want to trace the line of his cheekbone, run my fingers through his hair, pull his mouth down to mine.

But I can't.

The restraints hold me in place, spread open and helpless, unable to do anything but stare back at him while my body screams for contact.

"Are you dying for my cock, my pretty little slut?"

His voice is low and rough and it slides through me like warm honey.

I start nodding before I can think, the metal collar biting

into my throat with the movement. The pressure makes me gasp, but I don't stop.

"Yes, Master. Yes, Master, *please*. Let me have it. Give it to me."

His smile widens.

He doesn't give it to me.

Instead, he reaches out and traces one finger down the center of my chest, between my breasts, over my stomach, stopping just above my pussy. His touch is featherlight. Barely there. Enough to make every nerve ending in my body light up with desperate need but nowhere near enough to satisfy anything.

"Tell me how much you want it."

"So *much*," I breathe. "So *much*, Master. I've been thinking about it since the platform. Since you kissed me on the plank. I can't stop thinking about how you felt pressed against me, how hard you were, how badly I wanted you inside me right then."

"What would you do for it?"

"Anything." The word comes out without hesitation. "Anything you want. Whatever you tell me to do. I'll be good. I'll be so good for you."

His finger traces lazy circles on my lower stomach. Each pass brings him closer to where I need him, but he never quite arrives.

"You were good on the zip line," he says. "I watched you. Watched you conquer your fear. Watched you trust me enough to jump."

"I trusted you."

"I know." He leans closer, his breath warm against my ear. "I also watched you get wet listening to those voices describe what they wanted to do to you. Watched your pretty little pussy drip while they talked about fucking your throat and fisting your cunt."

My face burns.

"Did you like that?" His tongue traces the shell of my ear. "Did you like knowing they were watching you? Wanting you?"

"Yes," I whisper.

"Louder."

"Yes, Master. I liked it."

"You liked strange men looking at your naked body."

"Yes."

"You liked hearing them describe how they'd use you."

"Yes, Master."

"Would you let them?" His hand cups my breast, thumb brushing over my nipple. "If I gave permission? If I told you to spread your legs and let all three of them take turns?"

My pussy clenches hard enough that I feel it pulse.

"If you—if you wanted me to," I manage. "If it would please you."

"Such a good answer." He pinches my nipple, rolling it between his fingers until I cry out. "Such a perfect, obedient little slut."

He steps back.

I make a sound of protest that I'm immediately ashamed of—a desperate, needy whine that belongs to someone with no pride left.

But he just watches me with that knowing smile as his hands move to the buttons of his shirt.

He undoes them slowly. Deliberately. Making me watch each one reveal more of the chest beneath. The fabric parts to show tanned skin, defined muscle, and then—

Tattoos.

God, the tattoos.

They cover his torso in an intricate tapestry of images that makes my breath catch in my throat. I see curves, and shadows, and the woman who looks like me.

He shrugs the shirt off his shoulders and lets it fall to the jungle floor. His chest is a canvas of dark lines and careful shading, depicting scenes that feel hauntingly familiar. A woman bound. A woman kneeling. A woman with her head thrown back in ecstasy.

Me.

All of them are me.

The shirt drops and he reaches for his belt.

I watch his fingers work the buckle. Watch him pull the leather free with a slow, deliberate motion that makes me think about what that belt would feel like against my skin. He drops it beside the shirt.

His pants follow.

He's not wearing anything underneath.

His cock springs free—thick and hard and already leaking at the tip—and I make another desperate sound that I can't control.

"Look at me," he commands.

As if I could look anywhere else.

"Describe what you see."

My brain stutters.

"I—what?"

"You're a writer, aren't you?" He wraps his hand around his cock and strokes slowly from base to tip. "So write. Out loud. Describe me like I'm the hero of one of your stories."

The words catch in my throat.

He's standing in front of me, naked and gorgeous, his hand moving on his cock in lazy strokes while he waits for me to perform on command. The absurdity of it wars with the arousal flooding through my veins until I can't tell which one is winning.

"I—I don't—"

"You've written forty-seven stories about men like me." Another slow stroke. "You've described dominant men in exquisite detail. Their bodies. Their cocks. The way they command a room just by existing." His thumb swipes across the head, gathering the moisture there. "Now describe *me*."

I swallow hard.

My writer's brain kicks in almost against my will, cataloging details, building sentences, constructing the kind of prose I've spent years perfecting in the privacy of my blanket fort.

"The Masked Man," I begin, my voice shaking, "stands six-feet-three with shoulders broad enough to fill doorways and hands large enough to wrap completely around a woman's throat."

He smiles.

"His body is a study in controlled power—each muscle defined and deliberate, the kind of physique that comes from discipline rather than vanity. His chest is wide, tapering to a narrow waist, and every inch of his torso is covered in ink that tells stories I haven't yet learned to read."

His hand moves faster on his cock.

"His face is the face of a fallen angel—too beautiful to be human, too cruel to be divine. His eyes are dark pools that see everything, judge everything, desire everything. His jaw is sharp enough to cut glass and covered in stubble that leaves marks on soft skin. His lips are full and expressive, capable of delivering praise that makes a woman melt or commands that make her knees buckle."

"Keep going," he says. His voice is rougher now.

"His cock is—" I have to stop and breathe. "His cock is thick and long and curves slightly upward, the head flushed dark with blood and already wet with evidence of his arousal. It's the kind of cock that stretches a woman open, that fills her so completely she forgets where she ends and he begins."

My pussy clenches around nothing.

"The Masked Man is a dominant in the truest sense. He doesn't just take control—he *requires* it. He craves submission the way other men crave air, and he rewards it with a thoroughness that leaves his slaves wrung out and rebuilt."

His breathing is heavier now, his hand moving with purpose.

"He's demanding. Rough. He expects perfection and accepts nothing less. But he's not cruel for cruelty's sake—he's cruel because he knows his slaves need it. Because he understands that pain and pleasure are two sides of the same coin, and he's mastered the art of spending both."

"What else?" His voice is strained.

"He likes his slaves desperate," I continue, falling deeper into the fantasy. "He likes to edge them until they're sobbing, until they've forgotten their own names, until the only word left in their vocabulary is *please*. He likes to deny them and then reward them in measures so overwhelming they break apart in his hands."

His eyes never leave mine.

"And when he finally gives them his cock—when he finally fills them after hours or days of denial—he fucks them like he owns them. Because he does. Every orgasm belongs to him. Every moan. Every tear. Every confession whispered in the dark."

"And his slave?" he asks. "Describe her."

I feel my face flush even hotter.

"His slave is—she's—"

"You."

"I'm his slave," I whisper. "I'm small where he's large, soft where he's hard. I'm a writer who spent years putting her darkest fantasies on paper because she was too afraid to live them. I'm a mess of contradictions—desperate for control and terrified of it, craving submission and ashamed of wanting it."

He steps closer.

"I write stories about women like me," I continue, "women who get captured, and claimed, and owned by men like him. Women who find freedom in surrender. Women who discover that the cage they've built around themselves is the very thing keeping them from flying."

His hand falls away from his cock. He's standing right in front of me now, close enough that I can feel the heat radiating off his skin.

"And this story?" His voice is soft. Intimate. "The one you're living right now. What happens in this story?"

My heart is pounding so hard I can feel it in my throat.

"In this story," I say slowly, "the Masked Man finds a broken girl who's been hiding behind her words for too long. He sees through her defenses. He understands her darkness because he has darkness of his own. And instead of running from it—instead of being disgusted by the things she craves—he gives her exactly what she needs."

"Which is?"

"Everything." My voice breaks on the word. "He gives her everything. The pain she's too ashamed to ask for. The pleasure she's too afraid to accept. The safety of knowing someone else is in control, someone who won't leave, someone who sees her completely and stays anyway."

Silence stretches between us.

I'm exposed in ways that have nothing to do with my naked body spread on this cross. I've just recited my deepest fantasies to a man I barely know, performed like a trained pet while he stroked his cock and watched me struggle to find words worthy of what he makes me feel.

And I don't regret any of it.

Because somewhere in the middle of that description, I felt something shift. Something lock into place. The beginning of a story I've never written before—one where I'm not just the author, but the protagonist.

I'm going to write this.

I'm going to capture every moment of this experience in prose so vivid it burns. The terror and the arousal. The shame and the need. The way he looks at me like I'm something precious and the way he treats me like something owned.

The Masked Man will be the title. And unlike every other story I've written, this one won't be fiction.

His expression softens.

It's subtle—just a slight easing of the tension around his eyes, a gentling of his mouth—but it changes everything about the way he's looking at me. The predator is still there, lurking beneath the surface. But right now, in this moment, there's something else.

Something that almost looks like tenderness.

He reaches out and cups my face in both hands. "Good girl," he murmurs. "Such a good, *perfect* girl."

Then he kisses me.

Even gentler than the kiss from the platform. It's *so* soft, and *so* slow, and *so* thorough, his lips move against mine like he has all the time in the world. His tongue traces the seam of my mouth and I open for him instantly, desperate to let him in, desperate to give him whatever he wants.

He tastes like mint and something darker underneath. Something that makes me think of smoke, and whiskey, and late nights spent doing things I shouldn't.

His hands move from my face to my hair, fingers threading through the strands and tilting my head back to deepen the kiss. I moan against his mouth and he swallows the sound, giving me back a low growl of approval that vibrates through my chest.

This feels real.

It feels like more than just a scene, more than just a game he's playing with me. It feels like he means it—the tenderness, the care, the way he's kissing me like I'm something to be savored rather than consumed.

It feels like he wants me.

Not just my body spread open on this cross. Not just my submission and my desperate need. *Me.* The mess of contradictions, and shame, and hopeless romantic fantasies that I've been trying to hide my entire adult life.

When he finally pulls back, I'm breathless. Dizzy. My lips feel swollen and used in the best possible way.

He strokes his thumb across my cheekbone.

"Wait here," he says, and even though I literally cannot go anywhere, the command sends a shiver down my spine.

He turns and walks toward a cabinet I hadn't noticed before—built into the trunk of a massive tree about ten feet from the cross. It's dark wood, ornate, completely incongruous with the jungle setting around it.

He opens the doors.

Inside, I can see rows of implements hanging on hooks and arranged on shelves. Metal glints in the filtered sunlight. Leather coils. Things I recognize from pictures, and research, and the video of our last experience together.

Nipple clamps.

Floggers.

Crops.

Vibrators of various shapes and sizes.

Things I don't recognize at all—strange shapes and configurations that make my imagination run wild trying to figure out what they're for.

He takes his time selecting.

I watch his back—the muscles shifting beneath tattooed skin, the confident way he moves, the deliberate consideration he gives each item before choosing or discarding it. He's building anticipation. Making me wait. Making me wonder what he's going to do to me next.

The voices in the jungle have gone completely silent. There's no sound except the distant call of birds and the pounding of my own heart.

He turns back toward me with something in his hands.

I can't see what it is, he's holding it tight in his fist as he slowly approaches me.

My body tenses with anticipation. My pussy clenches. My nipples ache.

"Do you know what these are?" He holds up a pair of clamps connected by a delicate chain. The clamps themselves have small screws for adjusting tension, and the chain has weights hanging from its center.

I nod.

"Say it."

"Nipple clamps, Master."

"Do you remember when I put these on you after the auction?"

"No, Master."

"But you've written about them." It's not a question. He knows. He's read everything I've ever posted. "Twenty-three of your forty-seven stories include nipple clamps in some form. Usually adjustable. Usually weighted. Usually applied while the protagonist is restrained and unable to protect herself."

I swallow hard.

"You're going to feel them now," he says. "You're going to understand exactly what you've been making your characters endure."

He steps close enough that his bare chest nearly touches mine. His cock brushes against my hip—still hard, still wet at the tip—and I make a desperate sound that I can't control.

"Shh." He brushes his lips against my forehead. "Hold still."

His fingers find my right nipple.

He rolls it between his thumb and forefinger, working it until it's even harder than before, until it's a tight peak aching for more contact. The sensation shoots straight to my pussy, making me clench.

Then he attaches the clamp.

The pressure is immediate and intense—not quite pain, but close. A sharp bite that hovers right on the edge of too much. My breath catches in my throat and I arch against the restraints, but there's nowhere to go.

"Color?" he asks.

For a moment, I'm confused. Then I realize, he's asking if I need to safe word. He's asking if he can proceed.

"Green," I gasp. "Green, Master."

Keep going….

He moves to my left nipple.

Same treatment. Rolling and pinching until it's almost unbearably sensitive, then the bite of the clamp closing around it. The chain connecting them pulls taut across my chest, and the weights in the center swing gently with every breath I take.

Each swing tugs at both nipples simultaneously.

I whimper.

"Beautiful," he murmurs, stepping back to admire his work. "Absolutely fucking beautiful."

He returns to the cabinet.

This time when he comes back, he's holding a flogger—soft-looking leather falls attached to a braided handle. He runs the falls through his fingers, letting me watch the way they separate and come back together.

"You know what this is."

"Yes, Master."

"You've written about it."

"Yes, Master."

"Seventeen stories." He drags the falls across my stomach, the leather cool against my heated skin. "In seven of them, the flogger is used on the protagonist's breasts. In ten, it's used on her pussy. In three, both."

The leather trails lower.

"What do you want?" he asks.

I don't know how to answer. I want everything. I want nothing. I want him to make the choice so I don't have to be responsible for whatever comes next.

"Tell me," he commands. The falls brush against my inner thigh. "Be specific."

"I—I want—"

"Where do you want to feel this?" The leather traces the crease where my thigh meets my hip. "Here?"

I nod.

He brings the flogger back and swings it forward in a gentle arc. The falls connect with my inner thigh—not hard, just a soft thud of sensation that makes my skin tingle.

I moan.

"*More*," I beg. "Give me more. Make it harder. Make it… *hurt*."

CHAPTER 9
CALEB

Make it hurt.

Her words land somewhere between my chest and my cock, detonating on impact. The muscle in my jaw tightens. My dick throbs so hard it actually jumps, straining toward her like it has its own agenda, its own desperate need to be inside her.

She has no idea.

No fucking idea how much restraint I'm burning through right now. How every cell in my body is screaming at me to drop this flogger, grab her hips, and fuck her until she can't remember her own name. Until she can't remember anything except the feeling of my cock splitting her open.

Make it hurt.

I look her directly in the eyes.

Her pupils are blown so wide that her hazel irises have nearly disappeared, swallowed by black. The gold flecks I've memorized from a thousand hours of surveillance footage are invisible now, drowned in arousal and need and something that looks dangerously close to trust.

I can see my own reflection in those dark pools. A man holding a flogger. A man barely holding himself together.

"You should be very careful, my little slut, in what you ask for."

My voice comes out lower than I intended. Rougher. The predator bleeding through the controlled facade.

"Because we're writing this story together now." I let the words sink in, watching her face for any flicker of fear, any sign she's reaching for a safeword. "I'm not obligated to fulfill your wishes."

I bring the flogger back and swing it forward in a vicious arc, connecting solidly with her breasts.

The crack of leather against flesh echoes through the jungle clearing.

Scarletta gasps—loud, sharp, her whole body jerking against the restraints. The weighted chain between her nipple clamps swings wildly, tugging at both sensitive peaks simultaneously. Her back arches off the cross as much as the straps will allow, which isn't much.

Red blooms across her pale skin where the falls landed.

"I will be happy to hurt you," I continue, my voice steady even as my cock leaks precum against my thigh, "if you ask for it."

I step closer.

Close enough to feel the heat radiating off her flushed body. Close enough to smell her arousal mixing with the jasmine oil the attendants rubbed into her skin. Close enough to see the rapid flutter of her pulse in the hollow of her throat.

I cup her face in my free hand, tilting her chin up.

Then I kiss her.

Not a bruising, claiming kiss, but tender and slow. I trace the seam of her lips with my tongue, coaxing them apart, then slide inside to taste her properly. She moans into my mouth, and I swallow the sound, savoring it like whiskey.

I kiss her until her breathing changes.

Until the tension in her shoulders softens.

Until she's melting against me as much as her restraints

allow, surrendering into the gentleness after the sharp bite of pain.

I pull back just far enough to speak against her lips.

"I like to punish." The admission comes out quiet. Almost confessional. As close to vulnerable as I ever get.

"I like the way your skin reddens under my hand. I like the sounds you make when pleasure and pain blur together until you can't tell them apart. I like watching you struggle to process sensations you've only imagined, only written about, never actually felt."

I brush my thumb across her cheekbone, catching a tear I didn't realize had fallen.

"If you ask again," I tell her, "I will do it. I will hurt you exactly the way you need. Not to damage you. Not to break you. To give you what you've been craving since you started writing those stories. What you've been too afraid to ask for from anyone else."

I wait.

My cock is so hard now that it genuinely hurts, the ache spreading through my groin and into my lower back. Every second feels like an hour. Every heartbeat pounds through my skull like a countdown to something I can't name.

I wait for her answer.

I find myself doing something I haven't done since I was sixteen years old, standing on a balcony watching my mother's body fall toward the concrete below.

I pray.

Not to any god I believe in, because I don't believe in any of them. Not to the universe, which is indifferent at best and actively hostile at worst. I pray to whatever force brought Scarletta into my surveillance feeds six months ago. Whatever cosmic accident made her write the exact fantasies that have haunted my dreams since adolescence. Whatever twist of fate put her face on my body years before I knew she existed.

I pray she asks again.

The silence stretches between us, thick with tension and the distant sounds of the jungle. A bird calls somewhere in the canopy. The weights on her nipple clamps sway gently with her breathing, tugging at the sensitive flesh with each inhale.

Scarletta's tongue darts out to wet her lips.

She looks at me with those enormous dark eyes, her pupils still swallowing her irises, her cheeks flushed from arousal and the sting of the flogger.

"Hurt me."

Two words.

Two simple words that rearrange something fundamental in my chest.

I exhale slowly.

The breath I release feels like it's been trapped in my lungs for six months. Since the first time I read her stories. Since the first time I saw her face on my screen and recognized her as the woman already inked into my skin.

I step back from her.

My movements are deliberate now, measured, the predator's anticipation building in my bloodstream like a drug. I walk back to the cabinet, my bare feet silent on the platform, my cock bobbing obscenely with each step.

The flogger was a warm-up.

The flogger was kindergarten.

I set it aside and reach deeper into the cabinet, my fingers closing around what I actually need. The implements are organized by intensity, lowest to highest, and I bypass the beginner items entirely.

She asked me to hurt her.

I'm going to give her exactly what she asked for.

I pull out a cane.

Rattan. Thin. Flexible. The kind that whistles through the air before it connects, giving the recipient just enough warning to anticipate the pain but not enough time to prepare for it.

I've practiced with this cane for years. I know exactly how much force to use to leave a mark without breaking skin. I know the difference between a stroke that stings and a stroke that burns. I know how to layer pain on top of pain until the nervous system can't process individual sensations anymore, until everything blurs into a continuous wave of overwhelming input.

I turn back toward Scarletta.

Her eyes widen when she sees what I'm holding.

"Do you know what this is?" I ask, the same question I asked about the nipple clamps.

"A cane, Master." Her voice is smaller now. Less certain.

"Have you written about it?"

She nods.

"How many times?"

"I don't... I don't know exactly. Several."

"Eleven." I close the distance between us slowly, letting her watch me approach, letting her anticipation build with each step. "Eleven stories where your protagonists experience caning. In seven of them, the cane is applied to their ass while they're bent over furniture. In three, it's applied to their thighs while they're restrained standing. In one, it's applied to the soles of their feet."

I stop directly in front of her.

"You've researched it extensively. You've described the sound it makes. The way it leaves raised welts. The way the pain peaks several seconds after impact rather than immediately."

I drag the tip of the cane down her sternum, between her clamped breasts, over her stomach, lower.

"But you've never felt it."

"No, Master."

"You're going to feel it now."

I trace the cane along her hip, around to her thigh, down to her knee. Her skin pebbles with goosebumps in its wake.

"The flogger was a question," I tell her. "This is an answer."

I step to her side, positioning myself for optimal swing mechanics. The restraints hold her perfectly in place, her body stretched taut against the cross, every inch of her exposed and vulnerable.

I take a deep breath.

I adjust my grip on the handle, finding the perfect balance point.

I draw the cane back, measuring the distance, calculating the force.

And I wait.

I wait until her breathing quickens with anticipation.

I wait until her muscles tense involuntarily, bracing for impact.

I wait until she starts to relax again, thinking maybe I've changed my mind.

Then I swing.

The cane connects with both thighs simultaneously.

I feel the impact travel up the rattan, through my wrist, into my arm. The sound is exactly what I expected—that sharp whistle followed by a crack that echoes through the jungle clearing. I've practiced this stroke thousands of times on pillows, on hanging meat, on my own forearm once when I needed to understand what I was delivering.

Scarletta doesn't react immediately.

That's the nature of caning. The skin registers contact, but the nerve signals need time to travel, to be processed, to translate into conscious experience. I count in my head. One. Two.

Three.

She screams.

Not a cry. Not a gasp. A genuine scream that rips out of her throat and scatters birds from the nearby trees. Her entire body convulses against the restraints, pulling at the leather cuffs around her wrists, straining against the strap across her waist, her ankles jerking uselessly in their bonds.

Her head drops forward, chin hitting her chest.

I watch her carefully.

I watch the way her shoulders heave with each ragged breath. I watch the trembling that runs through her muscles like an electrical current. I watch the twin red lines already rising across her thighs, parallel welts that will darken over the next few minutes into perfect stripes.

Her hair has fallen forward, obscuring her face.

She's staring at the ground beneath the platform, her breathing loud and harsh in the sudden silence. The jungle seems to hold its breath around us, even the insects going quiet, as if the entire island is waiting to see what happens next.

I don't move.

I don't speak.

I let her process.

This is the critical moment. This is where I read every signal her body is transmitting and make the correct decision. If I see panic, genuine distress, the kind of fear that signals I've pushed too far, I'll stop everything. I'll release her from the cross, wrap her in my arms, carry her to the recovery station and spend the next hour in aftercare.

But that's not what I see.

Her breathing is slowing. Still ragged, still catching on each inhale, but slowing. Her shoulders are dropping from where they'd climbed toward her ears. Her hands, which had been clenched into fists inside the cuffs, are relaxing, her fingers uncurling.

And her thighs.

Her thighs are pressing together as much as the ankle restraints will allow, which isn't much. She's squeezing them, trying to create friction, trying to chase something.

I walk around the cross to face her.

My footsteps are deliberate, loud enough for her to track my movement. I don't want to startle her. I want her to know exactly where I am, exactly what I'm doing.

I stop directly in front of her.

She's still looking down, her hair a curtain between us.

I reach out and cup her chin, lifting her face.

Her eyes are wet. Tears track down her cheeks, leaving shiny trails on her flushed skin. Her lips are parted, swollen from where she's been biting them. Her pupils are still dilated, dark pools that seem to swallow the light.

She looks wrecked.

She looks beautiful.

I hold her gaze and slide my other hand between her legs.

My fingers find her pussy, and the wetness I encounter is obscene. She's drenched. Not just wet, but actively dripping, her arousal coating my palm the moment I make contact. Her inner thighs are slick with it, her pussy so swollen and hot that she feels almost feverish against my hand.

The cane did this to her.

The pain translated directly into arousal, exactly the way she's written about in her stories, exactly the way I knew it would.

I press two fingers against her clit.

She comes immediately.

No warning. No build-up. No gradual climb toward release. The orgasm hits her like a physical blow, her entire body seizing against the restraints as she cries out. Her pussy clamps down on nothing, rhythmic contractions I can feel against my palm as I cup her sex. Her hips jerk forward, chasing my hand, trying to grind against my fingers for more stimulation.

I don't move.

I keep my hand exactly where it is, providing steady pressure but nothing else, letting her ride out the orgasm on her own terms. I watch her face the entire time, cataloging every micro-expression, every flicker of pleasure and release that crosses her features.

She didn't ask permission.

I didn't give her permission.

She came without my consent, and I'm going to punish her for that. But underneath the cold calculation of discipline, something warm is spreading through my chest.

I was right.

I made the correct choice.

She wanted to be hurt. Not just tolerated it, not just endured it, but genuinely craved it. Her body's response is irrefutable proof. The orgasm that ripped through her seconds after the cane connected is evidence that I read her correctly, that I gave her exactly what she needed.

I've spent six months studying this woman. Six months watching her through hidden cameras, reading her stories before she posted them, learning every detail of her psychology through the fantasies she committed to paper. And now, standing in this jungle clearing with her come coating my fingers, I have confirmation that my obsession was justified.

I know her better than she knows herself.

Her orgasm finally subsides, the contractions slowing, her body going limp against the cross. The only things holding her up are the restraints. Without them, she'd be a puddle on the platform.

She hangs there for what feels like a long time.

Her breathing slowly steadies. The trembling in her muscles fades to occasional twitches. The flush on her chest begins to recede, though her cheeks stay pink.

I wait.

I'm patient. I've been patient for six months. I can be patient for another thirty seconds.

Finally, she lifts her head.

Her eyes find mine, and the expression on her face makes my cock throb painfully. She looks dazed, satisfied, wrecked—but there's something else underneath. Something hungry. Something that hasn't been sated despite the violent orgasm that just tore through her.

"More," she whispers.

One word. Barely audible. Her voice is hoarse from moaning.

"Please, Master. *More*."

The request hits me directly in the chest, spreading heat through my torso, down into my groin where my cock is already leaking steadily. She's asking me to hurt her again. After one strike, after coming so hard she couldn't hold herself up, she's asking for more.

I want to give it to her.

I want to paint her entire body with welts, to layer pain on top of pain until she's sobbing, and begging, and coming apart at the seams. I want to see how many times I can make her scream before she goes nonverbal. I want to push her to the absolute edge of what she can take and then hold her there, suspended in agony and ecstasy, until I decide she's had enough.

But not like this.

I set the cane aside, placing it on the equipment cabinet with deliberate care.

A proper caning requires proper positioning. She needs to be bent over a bench, her ass presented at the ideal angle for receiving strokes. Or strapped facing a tree, her back arched, her skin stretched taut. The cross is designed for different kinds of play—flogging, nipple torture, pussy torture, edging, denial.

I'm not done with her on the cross yet.

"No more cane," I tell her.

Her face falls, disappointment flickering across her features before she can hide it.

"Not tonight. Not like this." I gesture at her spread-eagle position. "When I cane you properly, you'll be bent over. You'll be presented. You'll be able to feel every stroke across your ass without the distraction of restraints pulling at your wrists."

I walk back to the cabinet.

I know exactly what I'm looking for. I've stocked this station with everything I might need, organized by sensation type and intensity. My fingers close around the handle of a wand vibrator, industrial strength, the kind that can force orgasms from even the most resistant body.

I turn back to face her, holding the vibrator where she can see it.

Her eyes widen.

"You came without permission."

My voice is flat. Controlled. The voice of a man about to deliver consequences.

"I didn't give you permission to come on my fingers. You took that orgasm without asking. That's theft, Scarletta. You stole something that belongs to me."

I flip the switch and the vibrator hums to life, a low buzz that fills the clearing.

"Do you know what happens to little sluts who steal?"

She shakes her head, though I suspect she already knows. She's written scenes like this. She's imagined exactly what I'm about to do to her.

"They get punished."

I step closer, close enough to press the vibrating head against her inner thigh, just inches from her swollen pussy.

"I'm going to make you come again."

I drag the vibrator higher, tracing a path through the wetness coating her skin.

"And again."

Higher still, until I'm circling her clit with the edge of the vibrating head, not quite making direct contact.

"And again."

I meet her eyes.

"Until you pass out."

Her breath catches.

"That's your punishment. Not denial. Not pain. Pleasure. So much pleasure your body won't be able to process it anymore. So many orgasms that you'll be begging me to stop, and I won't, because you didn't stop when I didn't give you permission."

I press the vibrator directly against her clit.

Her reaction is immediate, her hips jerking forward, a moan tearing from her throat. She's still so sensitive from the last orgasm that the stimulation must be almost painful.

"You're going to come for me over and over, until you can't stay conscious anymore. And when you wake up, you're going to remember that every orgasm belongs to me. Every time you come, it's because I allowed it. Because I chose to give it to you."

I increase the pressure slightly.

"Now be a good little slut and scream for me."

CHAPTER 10
SCARLETTA

The vibrator presses against my clit and the world narrows to a single point of sensation.

I'm already so sensitive from coming on his fingers, from the cane strike, from the flogger on my breasts. Every nerve ending is raw and exposed, screaming for relief and stimulation in equal measure. The buzz of the wand cuts through all of it, demanding my body's complete attention.

I come almost immediately.

My back arches against the cross, my wrists straining at the metal restraints, and my mouth falls open on a sound I don't recognize. It's not a moan or a scream, but something between the two. Something animal, and desperate, and entirely beyond my control.

"Good girl." His voice reaches me through the haze, distant but approving.

The orgasm crests and breaks and I'm gasping for air, my chest heaving, my thighs trembling in the restraints. But he doesn't move the vibrator. He keeps it pressed firmly against my clit, the relentless buzz continuing without pause.

No. No, it's too much, it's—

Another orgasm builds before the first one has even

finished receding. My body doesn't ask permission. My body doesn't care that I'm overstimulated, that my clit is swollen and aching, that every touch feels like electricity arcing through my nervous system. My body responds to the vibration the way it's designed to respond, clenching and releasing and climbing toward another peak whether I want it to or not.

I come again.

This time I do scream, the sound torn from my throat by the intensity of the sensation. My vision blurs at the edges, the jungle dissolving into smears of green and gold while his face remains sharp and focused in front of me. He's watching me fall apart. He's watching me lose control of my own body and he's not stopping.

You're going to come for me over and over until you can't stay conscious anymore.

His words echo in my mind as the third orgasm hits, rolling through me like a wave I can't outrun. My muscles are starting to cramp from the sustained tension. My lungs are burning because I keep forgetting to breathe between the spasms. My thoughts are fragmenting, scattering like papers in a wind I can't control.

This is when it happened before.

The recognition cuts through the pleasure-fog with sudden, sharp clarity.

This is when I started losing time.

I remember the auction. I remember the playroom. I remember coming so hard I blacked out, over and over, waking up in his lap with no memory of how I got there. He called it subspace psychosis afterward, gave me academic citations and clinical terminology, explained it as a documented phenomenon in deeply bonded power exchange relationships.

But I don't want that now.

I don't want to lose this. I don't want to wake up tomorrow and have gaps in my memory where this experience should be. I don't want to watch footage of myself on a screen like I did on Christmas morning, seeing my own face twisted in ecstasy while my conscious mind was somewhere else entirely.

I want to remember.

The fourth orgasm crashes through me and the blackness closes in at the edges of my vision. My body is responding without my mental input now, the way it did before, the physical mechanics of pleasure operating independent of my awareness. I can feel myself slipping, feel the dissociative fog creeping in, feel my consciousness trying to retreat from the overwhelming intensity.

No.

I force my eyes open.

The world is blurry and dark around the edges, but I find his face. I find his eyes. Blue-grey and watchful and fixed on me with an intensity that anchors me when everything else is spinning out of control.

"Red."

The word comes out broken. Barely audible over the buzz of the vibrator and my own ragged breathing. But it comes out.

He stops.

Immediately. Completely. The vibrator disappears from my clit and the sudden absence of stimulation is almost as overwhelming as the stimulation itself. My body keeps spasming, the orgasm still working through my muscles even though the source of it is gone, and I'm trying to breathe but I can't seem to remember how.

I'm hyperventilating.

I recognize the pattern from panic attacks I've had before, the rapid shallow breaths that don't actually deliver oxygen, the racing heart, the tingling in my fingers and toes. But this isn't panic. This is something else. This is my body trying to process more sensation than it was designed to handle.

"The blackness," I gasp out. "The—the thing you told me about—subspace—"

I can't get the words in the right order. They're coming out fragmented, tumbling over each other in my desperation to explain.

"I was losing time again. Like before. The dissociative—the fugue—I don't want to forget—"

The magnetic restraint opens from my right wrist, then my left. He crouches to release my ankles while I slump against the cross, my legs unable to hold me.

"I want to remember this," I manage, still breathing too fast. "I want to be able to—to think about it later—to write about it—I don't want gaps—"

He catches me as my knees buckle.

One moment I'm standing, barely, and the next moment I'm in his arms. He lifts me like I weigh nothing, one arm under my knees and the other supporting my back, and my head falls against his shoulder because I don't have the strength to hold it up anymore.

The weighted clamps are still on my nipples. I'd forgotten about them in the overwhelming intensity of the forced orgasms, but now I feel them swinging gently as he carries me down a trail. Each small movement sends a pulse of sensation through my breasts, a reminder that my body is still primed, and raw, and desperate.

Suddenly, as if time was missing, cool air hits my over-heated skin and I shiver violently, goosebumps erupting across my arms and thighs. The contrast with the humid jungle air is shocking, almost painful on nerves that are already over sensitized. But the cold helps. It cuts through the fog in my head, grounding me in physical reality instead of letting me drift.

The unmasked man sits down on a couch without releasing me.

I'm in his lap again. Like before. Like Christmas morning

when I woke up in this exact position with no memory of how I got there.

But this time I remember.

I remember the cross. The flogger. The cane. His cock pressing against my hip while I begged him for more. The forced orgasms and the blackness closing in and the word that stopped everything.

My breathing is still too fast, my body still trembling with aftershocks, but I'm *here*. I'm present. I'm conscious.

His fingers brush the hair from my forehead, gentle strokes that push the sweat-damp strands away from my face. The touch is soft in a way that doesn't match anything else that's happened today, and I find myself leaning into it without meaning to, my cheek pressing against his palm like a cat seeking warmth.

"This room was built specifically for moments like this," he says, his voice low and steady. "The temperature is calibrated to bring down core body heat gradually. The lighting mimics natural sunset wavelengths to encourage parasympathetic nervous system activation. The couch cushions are medical-grade memory foam designed to support post-scene physical recovery."

I'm looking up at him while he talks, watching the way his mouth forms the words, the way his jaw moves, the slight roughness along his cheekbones where stubble is starting to show. His eyes meet mine and something in them shifts, the clinical detachment giving way to something warmer and more uncertain.

"The ventilation system circulates air at precisely twenty-two degrees Celsius with forty percent humidity," he continues. "Optimal conditions for—"

He stops.

I realize he's describing technical specifications I'm not supposed to care about. He's giving me meaningless details about HVAC systems, and furniture materials, and lighting design because the words themselves don't matter.

What matters is his voice, the steady rhythm of it, the way it fills the silence and gives my fractured mind something to follow.

He's taking care of me.

The realization hits me somewhere deep in my chest, in a place that's been empty for so long I'd forgotten it existed. He's not expecting me to respond, or perform, or be anything other than what I am right now—which is a shattered mess of overstimulated nerve endings and confused emotions.

"Are you OK, Scarletta?"

The question is simple. His eyes search my face as he asks it, and I can see genuine concern there, genuine worry that he's pushed too hard, or taken too much, or damaged something that can't be repaired.

"I'm fine," I say automatically. The words come out before I can think about them, the reflexive reassurance I've been offering people my entire life. Don't worry about me. I'm fine. Everything's great. No need to concern yourself.

But I stop.

The lie hangs in the air between us, incomplete and obviously false, and I find myself asking the question I've been avoiding for as long as I can remember.

Am I OK?

Am I *actually* OK, or am I just saying what I think he wants to hear because that's easier than examining the truth? Am I fine, or am I so practiced at pretending to be fine that I've lost the ability to tell the difference?

The tears come before I can stop them.

They spill down my cheeks in hot streams, and I'm shaking my head no, no, I'm not OK, I'm not fine, I've never been fine, and the admission feels like pulling a thread that's been holding everything together for twenty-two years.

His face changes when he sees my tears. The concern

deepens into something that looks almost like sadness, like my pain is causing him pain, like he actually cares about my answer instead of just asking the question because it's what you're supposed to do after you've made someone come until they almost passed out.

But the unmasked man doesn't tell me I'm wrong.

He doesn't try to convince me that actually, I am OK, that I'm just being dramatic, that I'm overreacting to a perfectly normal experience.

He doesn't do what Derek used to do, which was dismiss my feelings as inconvenient obstacles to his own pleasure.

"Tell me," he says instead. "Explain it to me."

The words stick in my throat.

This is the part where I'm supposed to be good with words. This is the part where my supposed talent for language should kick in and help me articulate the tangled mess inside my head.

I've written forty-seven stories about women who feel exactly what I'm feeling right now, and I've found the perfect sentences to describe their shame, and their longing, and their desperate need to be understood.

But those were fictional women.

Those were characters I could control, puppets I could manipulate into saying exactly what needed to be said at exactly the right moment.

I'm not a character.

I'm a real person with real emotions that don't come with a backspace key, and right now I can barely string together a coherent thought.

"My whole life," I start, and my voice cracks on the second word. "My whole life I've felt like something was wrong with me."

He's watching me with total attention. Not the performative listening I've experienced from therapists, and counselors, and well-meaning teachers who were really just waiting for their turn to talk.

This is something different.

This is him actually hearing me, actually caring about what I'm trying to say.

"Even when I was little..." I force the words out through the tightness in my chest. "I *knew* I wasn't like the other kids. They could make friends so easily, just walk up to someone on the playground and start talking, and within five minutes they'd be best friends. I could never do that. I would watch them from the corner of the schoolyard, trying to figure out what they were doing differently, what secret social code they all understood that I couldn't crack."

The tears keep coming, but I don't try to stop them.

"My mother used to tell me I was too sensitive. Too much in my own head. She said I needed to stop daydreaming and start paying attention to the real world, but the real world never made sense to me the way the worlds inside my head did. The real world was loud, and confusing, and full of people who seemed to operate according to rules I couldn't understand."

He strokes my cheek with his thumb, wiping away tears that are immediately replaced by more.

"So I retreated. Into books, at first. Then into my own writing. I created characters who felt the things I felt, who wanted the things I wanted, and I gave them happy endings because I couldn't figure out how to get one for myself. And the more I retreated, the more disconnected I became from everyone around me, eventually, I just stopped trying to connect at all."

The words are tumbling out now, faster than I can organize them, a flood of confession that's been building for years.

"I hate myself," I whisper. "I've always hated myself. For being weird. For being different. For wanting things that nice girls aren't supposed to want. My mother found one of my stories once..."

I can't even finish as the memory floods in. My sobbing gets louder. The pain of that day, so real again.

The unmasked man caresses my cheek, paying attention to nothing but me. "You can do this, Scarletta," he whispers softly. "What happened when your mother found your story?"

I want to stop here. I want to pack up all my feelings and put them in a suitcase, then I want to lock that suitcase up and hide it under the bed.

But that's what I always do. And the thing no one tells you about packing your suitcase like that is... you have to take it with you, no matter where you go.

So instead... I find the courage to keep going. "She told me that good women don't think about sex, don't fantasize about being controlled, don't dream about being taken, and used, and owned. And I believed her. I believed that the darkness inside me was proof that something was fundamentally broken, that I was damaged goods, that no one would ever want me if they knew what I really was."

His hand cups my face, warm and steady.

"So I hid. I created ScarletSins and wrote all the things I couldn't say out loud, and for a while that was enough. I could pretend to be brave online while being invisible in real life. I could explore my darkness through fiction while maintaining the illusion that the real me was normal, and acceptable, and not a complete freak."

I'm shaking now, full-body tremors that have nothing to do with the temperature of the room.

"The cross was amazing," I manage. "It was everything I've ever written about and more. The pain and the pleasure and the feeling of being completely at your mercy, completely out of control. It was exactly what I've been fantasizing about for years."

I force myself to meet his eyes.

"And that's the problem. It was too good. So good that my brain couldn't reconcile how much I was enjoying it with everything I've been taught about what enjoying something like that means. The shame was eating me alive even while I was coming, and the only way my mind could handle it was to shut down completely. To black out. To escape into unconsciousness so I wouldn't have to face what I was feeling."

The admission hangs between us, raw and ugly and more honest than anything I've ever said to another human being.

"I was going to lose time again," I whisper. "Like I did at Christmas. Because my shame was too big to hold, and disappearing was easier than admitting how much I wanted everything you were doing to me. And I didn't want to do that. I don't want to watch myself experiencing your expert domination. I want to live it. I want to remember *everything*."

He's quiet for a long moment, his thumb still tracing gentle circles on my cheek, his eyes never leaving mine. Then he shifts slightly, adjusting his hold on me so I'm cradled more securely against his chest.

"You're beautiful," he says, and his voice is different now, softer somehow, like he's telling me something important instead of just offering a compliment. "Your face, the way your expressions change when you're processing something. Your body, the way it responds to my touch, the way your skin flushes, and your nipples harden, and your pussy gets wet when I'm barely touching you. Your tits, perfect handfuls that fit in my palms like they were made for me."

He pauses, and when he continues, his voice is even quieter.

"But the sexiest thing about you right now isn't any of that. The sexiest thing about you is that you just did the hardest thing a person can do. You looked inside yourself, found something ugly, and shameful, and terrifying, and you told me about it anyway. That takes more courage than anything I made you do on that cross."

I stare up at him, not quite believing what I'm hearing.

"I know what it feels like," he says. "The shame. The sense

that something inside you is fundamentally different from everyone else, fundamentally wrong. I grew up dreaming about delivering justice to people who escaped consequences. Not fantasy justice, not courtroom justice, but *real* justice. Permanent justice."

My brain registers what he's actually saying beneath the careful euphemisms.

He's talking about killing people.

He's talking about the way he killed Derek, tortured him for hours before dismembering and burning his body, because Derek raped me during a power exchange relationship and walked away without consequences.

I should be horrified.

I should be screaming, fighting to get away from this confessed murderer who's holding me in his lap like I'm something precious.

But I find myself leaning closer instead, pressing my ear against his chest to hear the steady rhythm of his heartbeat.

He senses that I'm listening, really listening, the way he listened to me. And something in his posture shifts, like he's been waiting for permission to tell me this, like my attention has unlocked something he's been holding back.

"It's called… The Scales. And it's… for me, anyway—" he's looking right into my eyes now, "—it's… *bliss*.

CHAPTER 11
CALEB

Scarletta's looking at me in a way no one has ever looked at me before.

Not with fear, though she should be afraid.

Not with judgment, though I've just handed her every reason to condemn me.

She's looking at me with recognition, like she's found a puzzle piece that finally fits into the jagged hole she's been carrying around her whole life.

I understand her shame because I've lived with my own version of it since I was old enough to understand that the thoughts inside my head weren't normal.

"I always knew I was different too," I tell her, and the words feel strange in my mouth, foreign, like a language I stopped speaking years ago. "Even as a kid. The other boys were obsessed with baseball cards, and video games, and whatever cartoon was popular that week. I was obsessed with the news."

Scarletta's lips curve into a small smile, the first genuine expression of lightness I've seen from her since she safe-worded. The sight of it does something complicated to my chest, a warmth spreading through tissue I'd assumed was calcified beyond repair.

I find myself returning the smile, which is its own kind of revelation. Smiling is not something I do. Smiling is a social performance, a mask people wear to signal approachability, and I've never had any interest in being approached.

But this smile happens without my permission, pulled from somewhere deep by the simple fact of her amusement.

"Yes, fine," I admit. "A child obsessed with the news is objectively strange. I'm aware of how that sounds. But it wasn't the politics that drew me in, though there was certainly a political component to what I was noticing. And it wasn't the crime itself, though crime was at the center of everything."

I pause, organizing my thoughts into something coherent, something that will make her understand the architecture of the man holding her.

"It was the injustice," I say. "Watching people get hurt with no consequences for the ones who hurt them. Just victims. Victims everywhere I looked, on every channel, in every newspaper my father left scattered around the house. Children who disappeared and were never found. Women who were assaulted and watched their attackers walk free. Families destroyed by drunk drivers who served six months and went back to their lives like nothing happened."

Scarletta's body has gone still against mine, her breathing shallow as she listens.

"Somewhere along the line, the police stopped being about finding criminals and stopping them from hurting more people. They became revenue generators, traffic stop quotas, civil asset forfeiture machines. The legal system stopped being about weighing evidence and finding truth, and started being about who could afford the better lawyer, who had connections to the judge, who could drag proceedings out until witnesses died, or gave up, or forgot."

I can hear the anger bleeding into my voice now, the cold fury that's been burning in my chest since I was twelve years old and watched a man who'd molested four children walk out of a courtroom because the prosecutor made a procedural error.

"America has a third-world justice system," I tell her. "We pretend otherwise because we have marble courthouses and Latin phrases carved above the doors, but the reality is that criminals with money walk free while their victims live in fear for the rest of their lives. The scales of justice aren't balanced. They're bought and sold to the highest bidder."

Scarletta's hand moves against my chest, not pushing away but pressing closer, like she's trying to absorb the vibration of my anger through her palm.

"My grandfather left me a trust fund," I continue. "It wasn't my father's money, which meant my father couldn't touch it, couldn't control me with it the way he controlled everything else in my life. I used that money to start an investment firm while I was still at Harvard. Venture capital, private equity, finding undervalued companies and either buying them outright, or taking strategic positions that gave me leverage."

I watch her face as I explain the mechanics of my wealth, looking for the flicker of greed or calculation that I've learned to expect from people who discover what I'm worth. I don't find it. She's listening to understand me, not to assess my value as a resource.

"I was a billionaire by twenty-eight," I say. "Self-made, more or less. The trust fund gave me the initial capital, but I multiplied it by a factor of forty through my own decisions, my own analysis, my own willingness to make moves that other investors were too cautious or too stupid to make."

I pause, letting the weight of what I'm about to say settle between us.

"That's when I started The Scales."

Scarletta doesn't flinch. She doesn't pull away or ask me to stop talking. She waits, her body warm and trusting against mine, her attention completely focused on the words coming out of my mouth.

"It was a way to redirect the anger," I explain. "All that fury I'd been carrying since childhood, all that impotent rage at a system designed to protect the powerful at the expense of the weak. I could either let it poison me from the inside. or I could channel it into something productive. Something that would actually make a difference."

I think about the network I've built over the past few years, the other men who share my particular moral clarity, the resources we've pooled to ensure that the worst predators don't escape consequences simply because they can afford better lawyers than their victims.

"Derek was an indulgence," I admit, and I feel a small flicker of something that might be embarrassment at the confession. "He's not the kind of target I usually pursue. The Scales is reserved for the most dangerous predators, the ones who operate at scale, the ones whose wealth and influence make them untouchable by conventional means. Child traffickers. Serial rapists who buy off prosecutors. Men who've built empires on human suffering and convinced the world they're philanthropists."

Scarletta's breathing has changed, deeper and slower, like she's processing what I'm telling her at a level beneath conscious thought.

"Derek was personal," I continue. "He was small, insignificant in the grand scheme of the evil I've dedicated my resources to eliminating. But he touched you. He *hurt* you. He violated your trust and your body, and then walked away like you were nothing, like what he did to you didn't matter."

I feel my jaw tighten at the memory of what I found when

I started investigating him, the pattern of women he'd manipulated and assaulted under the guise of BDSM education, the trail of psychological damage he'd left in his wake.

"I don't regret what I did to him," I say. "If anything, I regret that I couldn't make it last longer. But I'll admit that it was an emotional decision, which is not something I typically allow myself. Emotion clouds judgment. Emotion creates mistakes. The Scales works because it operates on logic, on evidence, on careful verification that every target has genuinely earned the justice we deliver."

I think about Volk on the sister island, the real reason I'm here this week, the monster whose suffering I've been monitoring on the secondary screen wall while I've been orchestrating Scarletta's pleasure.

By now the fire ants have likely done their work. The venom builds in the bloodstream, attacking the cardiovascular system, causing tissue necrosis and systemic shock. If he's not dead already, he's very close.

The cameras were glitching earlier, the footage degrading in ways I couldn't immediately explain, but the biometric tracker showed his heart rate spiking into dangerous territory before I left the control room to come to Scarletta.

Dimitri Volkov built an empire on the bodies of trafficked children. He funded orphanages as recruitment centers, used his shipping company to move human cargo across borders, bought politicians, and prosecutors, and police commissioners to ensure his operation remained invisible to anyone who might interfere.

His death won't bring back the children he destroyed. It won't undo the trauma of the survivors who escaped his network. But it will stop him from hurting anyone else, and it will send a message to others like him that money and influence can't protect them from the consequences they've earned.

That's what The Scales is for.

That's the bliss I mentioned to Scarletta, the particular satisfaction of watching a predator realize that his power means nothing, that all the resources he accumulated to shield himself from accountability have failed him completely.

She's still pressed against my chest, still listening to my heartbeat, still processing everything I've told her. I wait for the questions I know are coming, the horror that should be dawning in her eyes, the realization that she's naked in the arms of a man who tortures and kills people and calls it justice.

But she doesn't pull away.

She doesn't scream.

She just breathes, slow and steady, her body relaxed against mine like she's found somewhere safe to rest.

The air in the aftercare room feels different now, charged with something I can't quite name. I've just confessed to being a serial killer with a moral code, and she's lying against my chest like I told her I enjoy stamp collecting.

I exhale slowly, the breath carrying more weight than it should.

"I get it," I tell her, and I mean it in a way that surprises me. "The shame you described, the feeling of being fundamentally broken because of what goes on inside your head. I feel it too."

My hand moves through her hair without conscious decision, the strands sliding through my fingers like water.

"I'm probably insane," I admit, and the words taste strange in my mouth because I've never said them out loud before. I've thought them, certainly. I've run the diagnostic criteria in my head late at night when the satisfaction of a completed hunt starts to fade and I'm left alone with the reality of what I've done. But speaking them to another person feels like removing a piece of armor I didn't realize I was wearing.

Scarletta doesn't respond, but her breathing remains steady against my chest. She's still here. Still listening.

"If you'd like to leave," I continue, and something tightens in my gut as I say it, "I'll take you back to the preparation pavilion. Give you a private room. You can clean up, eat something, rest for as long as you need. Then I'll put you on a plane home."

I watch her face for any flicker of relief, any sign that she's been waiting for permission to escape the madman who's been holding her.

"The money will be in your account regardless," I add before she can answer. "The full fifty thousand base pay, plus the bonuses you earned at Stations One and Two. You've more than fulfilled your contractual obligations."

The silence stretches between us.

I'm not accustomed to uncertainty. I plan every variable, anticipate every outcome, maintain control over situations through sheer force of preparation and will. But right now, watching Scarletta process everything I've told her, I find myself genuinely unable to predict what she's going to say.

It's uncomfortable.

It's also, I realize with some surprise, almost exhilarating.

She still hasn't spoken, so I continue. Part of me recognizes that I'm making a pitch, selling her on something, which is absurd because I've never had to sell anyone on anything. I acquire what I want through planning and resources, not persuasion.

But here I am, laying out options like a salesman with a quota.

"If you stay," I tell her, "I've got eight more stations set up for you. Designed them myself. Every detail calibrated to the specific fantasies you've written about, the particular psychological triggers I've identified in your work."

I pause, letting the weight of that settle.

"Station Three is exceptional," I say, and I can hear something almost like enthusiasm bleeding into my voice. "A maze in the jungle. Sensory deprivation. Complete trust required. The psychological intensity exceeds anything we've done so far."

Scarletta's lips curve slightly at the corners, and the sight of it loosens something in my chest.

"Then a break for lunch," I continue. "It's Valentine's Day, after all."

She smiles properly now, a small sound escaping her throat that might almost be called a giggle. The sound is so unexpected, so completely incongruous with the heavy confessions we've been trading, that I find myself staring at her like she's a species I've never encountered before.

"I had the kitchen prepare something special," I tell her. "Fresh seafood brought in this morning. Lobster, oysters, whatever you want. The chef trained at a three-star restaurant in Paris before I hired him away with an offer he couldn't refuse."

I'm rambling now, which is not something I do. Caleb MacLeay does not ramble. Caleb MacLeay speaks with precision and purpose, every word calculated for maximum impact.

But Scarletta is watching me with that small smile still playing at the edges of her mouth, and I find myself wanting to keep talking just to see if I can make it grow.

"After lunch, two more stations," I continue. "Then a full massage, a proper bath with the attendants, and dinner. I was thinking the terrace overlooking the ocean. Sunset should be spectacular this time of year."

I hesitate for a moment, weighing whether to reveal the next part. But I've already told her I kill people for justice. Admitting that I want her company seems almost trivial by comparison.

"I was going to invite you to sleep in my room tonight," I say, and I'm aware that my voice has dropped lower, softer, into a register I don't typically use. "Not for sex. Obviously we've had all the sex we need for one day."

The understatement hangs in the air between us, and I see her eyes flicker with amusement at the absurdity of it.

"But for companionship," I finish. "I thought it might be... pleasant. To not be alone."

The word feels inadequate. Pleasant is what I call a well-executed business deal or a satisfying meal. It doesn't capture whatever this thing is that's happening in my chest, this strange warmth spreading through tissue I'd assumed was incapable of feeling anything beyond satisfaction at a hunt well-conducted.

"Then tomorrow," I continue, because she still hasn't responded and the silence is starting to feel like a physical weight pressing against my lungs, "five more stations. Each one progressively easier, not harder. A gradual descent rather than an escalating climb. We'd be finished by lunchtime."

I think about the beach on the eastern shore of the island, the white sand and clear water I've never actually used because I'm always too busy monitoring operations and planning hunts.

"After that, we could do something fun," I say, and the word sounds foreign in my mouth. Fun is not a concept I typically apply to my existence. "Go to the beach. Swim. There's a boat if you want to go out on the water. Fishing equipment if that appeals to you. Whatever you want."

I stop talking because I've run out of things to offer her.

The silence returns.

Scarletta is looking at me with an expression I can't quite parse, her eyes searching my face for something I'm not sure I'm capable of providing.

I wait for her answer.

And wait.

And realize, with a sensation that feels disturbingly like vertigo, that I don't know what she's going to say.

This is not a familiar feeling. I research. I plan. I anticipate outcomes and prepare contingencies for every possible scenario. But Scarletta exists outside my models, unpredictable in ways that my usual methods of analysis can't account for.

I think about what happens if she chooses to leave.

The plane ride back to Idaho Falls. The empty apartment waiting for her, still decorated with the Christmas tree I had installed, still monitored by cameras she hasn't disabled. She'll write about this experience eventually. She'll turn it into another story for her readers, another chapter in the ongoing narrative of ScarletSins and her dark fantasies.

And I'll be here.

Alone.

Watching her through screens, reading her words, cataloging her patterns, but never touching her again.

The thought produces a physical reaction in my chest, a tightening sensation that I identify after a moment as something I haven't experienced in years.

I'm going to be sad if she leaves.

The realization lands like a blow.

I don't do sad.

I do focused. I do driven. I do satisfied when a hunt concludes successfully and empty when I'm between targets. But sad implies caring, implies investment, implies that this woman has somehow become more than a project, more than an obsession, more than the subject of six months of careful surveillance and planning.

I look at her face, at the way the soft lighting of the aftercare room catches the gold flecks in her hazel eyes, at the small smile that hasn't quite faded from her lips.

I want her to stay.

Not because I've invested resources in this operation.

Not because her departure would represent a failed mission.

I want her to stay because the thought of watching her walk away makes something inside me feel hollow in a way I don't have words for.

She still hasn't answered.

CHAPTER 12
SCARLETTA

He just told me he kills people.

Not hypothetically. Not metaphorically. He runs an organization called The Scales that hunts down wealthy predators who escape justice and makes them suffer.

I should be horrified.

I should be calculating the distance to the nearest exit, mapping escape routes in my head, wondering if I can outrun him through the jungle and signal for help.

That's what a normal person would do.

That's what the protagonist in any rational thriller would be doing right now—cataloging weapons, assessing threats, preparing to fight for her survival.

But I'm not thinking about any of that.

I'm thinking about how… I've *never* had a Valentine's Day date.

The absurdity of this hits me like a slap, and I almost laugh out loud at myself. Here I am, sitting in the lap of a confessed professional killer, naked, and exhausted, and still slightly trembling from the aftershocks of multiple forced orgasms, and my brain has decided to fixate on the romantic implications of his invitation.

Eight more stations. A jungle maze. Seafood lunch and a massage. Ocean-view dinner. Sleeping in his room—not for sex, he said. For companionship.

This is, objectively, the most elaborate Valentine's Day date anyone has ever planned for me.

This is the *only* Valentine's Day date anyone has ever planned for me.

I think about what this would look like on social media. The aesthetic perfection of it all—the tropical island, the candlelit aftercare room, the handsome man with his careful touches and his knowledge of exactly what I need. I could film reels that would make women around the world spiral with jealousy. *Look at my Valentine's Day date! He built an entire scavenger hunt just for me! He knows all my fantasies and makes them come true!*

The torture confession.

The corporate-funded executions.

The methodical way he explained Derek's death like discussing dinner plans.

All minor details.

I almost do laugh then, a small sound that escapes before I can stop it. The unmasked man looks at me with concern, probably wondering if I'm having some kind of psychological break.

Maybe I am.

Or maybe I'm just finally accepting that nothing is what it seems. That the most romantic gesture anyone has ever made for me comes wrapped in darkness, and blood, and the kind of moral complexity that would give philosophers nightmares.

That the person who sees me most clearly, who understands my writing, and my shame, and my desperate need to be known, is someone the world would call a monster.

I wonder if that makes me insane too.

I picture what tonight would look like. This tall, handsome, muscular, competent man—and he is all of those things, objectively beautiful in ways I still haven't fully processed—sitting beside me on a couch. We might watch movies. Something mindless and easy, the kind of film I've seen a hundred times because I needed the comfort of knowing how it ends.

Or we might play board games. Yahtzee or Scrabble or something ridiculous that would make me laugh.

We might take a walk on the beach in the moonlight, and he might point out constellations, and I might pretend I know anything about astronomy beyond what I've researched for stories.

And then, once the evening was over, I'd be in his bed.

Not for sex. He was clear about that.

For companionship.

He might hold me.

The thought sends something through my chest that I don't have a name for. Something that aches in the best possible way, sharp and sweet and terrifying all at once.

When was the last time someone *held* me?

Not touched me, not fucked me, not used my body for their pleasure—but actually *held* me?

Just the simple act of arms around me, warmth against my back, another heartbeat close enough to feel?

I can't remember.

I look up at him, at the face I'm still not used to seeing without the mask. The strong jaw and the careful eyes and the way he watches me like I'm the most important thing in his universe.

"Tell me about Station Three," I say.

Something shifts in his expression. Interest, maybe. Enthusiasm. He straightens slightly, and I recognize the posture of someone who's about to sell me on something they believe in.

"It's a maze," he says. "In the jungle. Your attendants will be inside—the same men from the bathing station, though you won't recognize them with their masks. You'll have to navigate through, and they'll be hunting you. If they get you, Scarletta, they'll make you come. Then…"

I laugh a little. "Then you'll have to punish me."

"I'll have to punish you, my dirty little slut. And it will be a punishment you'll recognize." He actually waggles his eyebrows at me.

I nearly come undone with laughter. But the promise he just made—a punishment I will recognize—means it's something I've written.

The idea is both delicious and terrifying. Because I've come up with some pretty challenging punishments for my leading ladies.

Punishments that sound erotic on the page—but in real life would be… *intense.*

I should be alarmed by this. The idea of being chased through a jungle maze by masked men should trigger every survival instinct I possess.

Instead, my pulse picks up in a way that has nothing to do with fear.

"You like mazes," he continues, and there's a hint of a smile playing at the corners of his mouth. "I've read your stories. The chase scenes are always the most vivid, the most detailed. You write them with a kind of joy that's different from your other work."

He's right. I do like mazes. I've always liked them—the puzzle of them, the way they require you to think and adapt and find your way through. And the chase scenes in my stories have always been my favorites to write. The fear, and the adrenaline, and the desperate hope of escape or capture, depending on what the protagonist wants.

"It's the most demanding of the stations," he says. "Four and five are more straightforward after that. More purely kinky, less psychologically complex. But Station Three is meant to be a trust-builder."

He pauses, and his eyes meet mine with an intensity that makes my breath catch.

"You'll emerge feeling exhilarated," he says. "Proud of yourself. You'll know that you can face something that scares you and come out the other side stronger for it."

I think about all the times I've written heroines who faced impossible challenges and discovered reserves of courage they didn't know they possessed. I think about how I've always admired them from a distance, wishing I could be that brave, that resilient, that capable of rising to meet whatever the world threw at them.

Maybe this is my chance to find out if I can.

"OK," I say. "I'll finish the day."

The relief that flickers across his face is subtle, but I catch it. He wanted me to stay. The realization warms something inside me that I didn't know was cold.

"I'm really hungry," I admit, because now that the decision is made, my body is reminding me of all its other needs. "And I need to pee. Badly."

The shift in his demeanor is almost comical. He goes from intense and earnest to practical and accommodating in the space of a heartbeat, standing up with me in his arms, then setting me down carefully. Like I'm something precious that might break.

Ironic for a man who whipped me with a cane thirty minutes ago. The evidence of which is still burned across the front of my thighs in bright red welts.

"Bathroom's through there," he says, directing me toward a door on the far side of the room. "Take all the time you need. There's water in the fridge, and I left food for you— cheese, fruit, some other things. Eat as much as you want. Station Three will wait."

I nod and take a step, my legs still slightly unsteady as I cross the room. The bathroom is as carefully designed as everything else on this island—clean lines, soft lighting, expensive fixtures. I close the door behind me and lean against it for a moment, just breathing.

I'm going to finish the day.

I'm going to navigate a jungle maze while masked men hunt me. As they try to make me come while I try and resist.

I'm going to sleep in his bed tonight, and he might hold me.

I'm spending Valentine's Day with a serial killer who knows my darkest secrets and thinks I'm exceptional.

I start laughing. Quietly at first, then harder, until tears are streaming down my face and I'm not sure if I'm laughing or crying or both. The sound echoes off the tile walls, and I let it happen, let the hysteria work its way through my system until I'm empty and calm again.

Then I pee, wash my hands, splash water on my face, and look at myself in the mirror.

I look different. Something in my eyes has changed. I look like someone who's been through something and survived it. I look like someone who might actually be brave.

I look like one of my heroines.

When I emerge from the bathroom, he's gone.

The aftercare room is empty except for the lingering warmth of his presence and the quiet hum of the climate control system. I stand there for a moment, absorbing the silence, then make my way to the refrigerator he mentioned.

Inside, I find water bottles, a selection of cheeses arranged on a wooden board, fresh fruit cut into bite-sized pieces, crackers, and some kind of cured meat. It's the kind of thoughtful, curated spread that someone puts together when they want to make sure you have options without overwhelming you with choices.

He thought about this. About what I might need in the middle of the experience.

This isn't a lunch or a dinner, but a *break*.

He planned for my break. For my safe word.

I don't even know how to process this so... I just eat slowly, savoring each bite. The cheese is sharp and creamy, the fruit perfectly ripe, the water cold and clean. I hadn't realized how hungry I was until I started eating, and now my body demands more with an urgency that surprises me.

By the time I'm finished, I feel almost human again. Restored. Ready.

I walk to the door of the aftercare station, take one last look at the room where I broke down crying and confessed things I've never told anyone, and step outside.

The jungle greets me with its wall of heat and green and the constant symphony of insects and birds. The air smells like flowers and rain and something else underneath—earth, maybe, or the sea.

There's a card pinned to a tree directly in front of me.

I pull it off the nail and turn it over, reading the poem...

Footsteps echo, jungle deep,
    Naked skin meets morning air.
    Follow pathways, do not weep,
    Station Three awaits you there.

Headphones fastened, blindfold tight,
    Darkness guides your senses keen.
    Jungle whispers, day to night,
    Commands will flow, like a stream.

Run now wildly, breathe the thrill,
    Chase begins when you take flight.
    Hunters prowl with practiced skill,
    Seeking pleasures you won't fight.

• • •

Listen closely, heed each word,
>   Though temptation bids you stray.
>   Every order must be heard—
>   Or the hunters win their prey.

Failure brings the prize you crave,
>   Punishment you long to feel.
>   Play the victim, play the brave,
>   All your fantasies made real.

Maze of pleasure, maze of play,
>   Rules you wrote, brought to life.
>   Valentine's most thrilling day,
>   Caught between surrender's strife.

Master waits at journey's end,
>   Knowing well your heart's desire.
>   Every capture, twist and bend,
>   Feeds your body's growing fire.
>   I stop breathing.

The card trembles in my fingers as I read the poem twice, three times. I blink. Swallow. My throat clicks audibly in the humid jungle air.

I know this story.

Not just *know* it—I *wrote* it. Every word. Every scene. Every brutal, unforgivable moment.

The Call of the Labyrinth.

Lyra and Helix.

My hands are shaking so badly now that the card blurs in front of my eyes. I read it again, confirming what I already know, what my body recognized before my brain caught up.

Lyra was a human woman kidnapped from her world.

Dragged into darkness by Helix, a horned monster-man from a cursed underground realm. He claimed she was his destined mate, but first she had to prove herself worthy through the Labyrinth—an ancient trial that would determine if she deserved to stand beside him.

He told her a portal waited at the maze's center. That if she reached it, she could go home.

It was a lie.

There was no portal. There was never any escape. She was trapped in his world permanently, and the trial existed only to break her down until she accepted her captivity as salvation.

The maze wasn't empty. Three animalistic monsters hunted her through the twisting corridors—Helix's enemies who viewed human females as breeding stock. If they caught her, she faced violation, captivity, repeated assault as a slave-breeder until her body gave out.

Helix's voice guided her through telepathic bond. Short-cuts. Portal-jumps. Instructions she had to follow blindly even when every survival instinct screamed to run the other way.

She was captured three times.

The first capture—tackled and pinned, the monster gloating over his prize while she struggled uselessly beneath him. She escaped only because Helix's voice directed her toward a nearby portal-arch. She rolled through it mid-assault, teleporting away before he could finish what he started.

The second capture—caught and dragged toward a breeding chamber while she screamed and fought. She escaped by deliberately triggering a maze trap Helix warned her about. The collapsing wall separated her from her captor, crushed his reaching arm, gave her time to flee.

The third capture—restrained and violated while she went somewhere far away in her head. She escaped only because the monsters began fighting over who would get her next. Their violent dispute gave her the opening she needed to slip free and run.

Each escape showed her growing trust in Helix's guidance despite mounting trauma. Each capture stripped away another layer of resistance until she was raw and desperate and willing to accept any hand that offered help.

Lyra reached the center broken. Discovered the portal was a lie. Found Helix waiting to heal her, claim her, keep her forever.

The lesser evil.

But still captivity.

I wrote this story when I was eighteen years old. Freshman year of college, living in my cramped dorm room with a roommate who thought I was studying late when really I was pouring my darkest fantasies onto the page. I didn't know the rules back then. I didn't understand that certain things couldn't be written, that certain lines couldn't be crossed even in fiction.

I thought I could write anything.

The monsters in my maze didn't ask permission. They didn't negotiate. They took what they wanted because that was the point—the terror, the helplessness, the desperate relief when Helix's voice cut through the darkness and showed Lyra the way out. The contrast made him seem safe by comparison. The trauma bonded her to him more effectively than any kindness ever could.

I was so proud of that story. Forty-seven thousand words of pure psychological horror wrapped in erotic fantasy. It felt real in a way nothing I'd written before had felt real. It felt like I'd finally excavated something true about myself and put it on the page.

Just before I published it, I saw a post on DarkDesires. Someone had gotten their book banned from Amazon for non-consent content. The comments were full of warnings

—dub-con will get you flagged, non-con will get you removed entirely, even fantasy rape in fantasy settings with fantasy creatures can trigger takedowns if it's too explicit.

I read that post three times, cold dread spreading through my chest.

Then I looked at what I'd written.

The Call of the Labyrinth wasn't dub-con. It wasn't even non-con with plausible deniability. It was three graphic assault scenes played for terror and titillation, a heroine who survived through dissociation and learned helplessness, a hero whose only virtue was that he hurt her less than the alternatives.

It was unpublishable.

It violated every standard, every guideline, every unspoken rule that made dark erotica acceptable. Even Dark-Desires—a second-rate Literotica knockoff where anything supposedly went—would have banned me for posting it.

I never published *The Call of the Labyrinth*.

I buried it in a folder on my hard drive labeled "OLD DRAFTS - DO NOT OPEN" and tried to forget I'd ever written it. Tried to forget what it said about me that I'd spent weeks crafting those scenes, that I'd made myself wet writing Lyra's terror, that I'd come harder reading her third capture than I ever had in real life.

But the unmasked man has access to my computer.

He's been inside my hard drive for six months. He's read everything I've ever written—not just the stories I posted on DarkDesires, but the drafts, the abandoned projects, the shameful attempts I never showed anyone.

He found it.

He found the darkest thing I've ever created, the story I was too ashamed to share even anonymously, and he built a real-life version of it in the middle of a tropical jungle.

For me.

For Valentine's Day.

I'm going to be sick.

I lean against the tree and press my forehead to the rough bark, breathing through my nose in shallow gasps. The humid air feels like it's choking me. Sweat drips down my spine and pools at the small of my back where I'm still naked, still exposed, still vulnerable in ways I can't seem to escape no matter how many times I think I've adjusted.

Can I do this?

That's the question, isn't it? The only question that matters right now.

Can I walk into a maze knowing what waits for me inside? Can I let myself be hunted by the same men who touched me at the bathing station, who made me come without permission, who know exactly how my body responds to their hands? Can I be captured, and used, and violated the way I wrote Lyra being violated?

Can I trust his voice to guide me through?

I think about the girl I was at eighteen. The one who wrote Lyra's story because she needed somewhere to put all the darkness inside her, all the shameful wanting that had no acceptable outlet. She didn't know what any of it meant. She just knew that the fear, and the helplessness, and the desperate relief felt *real* in a way nothing else did.

She knew that Lyra's surrender wasn't weakness.

It was survival.

I think about what the unmasked man said in the aftercare room. About how Station Three was designed as a trust-builder. About how I would emerge feeling exhilarated and proud, knowing I could face something that scared me and come out stronger.

He wasn't talking about a simple maze.

He was talking about this.

About *The Call of the Labyrinth* made flesh.

About walking into my darkest fantasy and discovering whether I could survive it.

Whether I could trust him enough to let it play out.

My fingers find the raised welts across my thighs where the cane struck me. The pain has faded to a dull throb, but when I press against the tender skin, it flares back to life—sharp, immediate, grounding.

I wrote that punishment too.

I wrote all of this.

Every fantasy I've ever committed to paper, every dark desire I've explored through fiction, every scenario I thought was too extreme to ever happen in real life—he's turning them into reality.

He's giving me exactly what I asked for.

The question is whether I'm brave enough to accept it.

I read the poem one more time.

Hunters prowl with practiced skill, seeking pleasures you won't fight.

Failure brings the prize you crave, punishment you long to feel.

All your fantasies made real.

I fold the card carefully and hold it against my chest, feeling my heart pound against the paper.

Then I start walking toward Station Three.

CHAPTER 13
CALEB

The afternoon light on Story Island has always possessed a peculiar quality that I've come to appreciate during my years of owning this place—dappled sunlight filtering through the dense canopy overhead, breaking apart into scattered beams that pierce the shadows below like scattered messages from some divine entity.

The effect is almost theatrical, the way the light shifts and dances, creating dramatic contrasts of illumination and darkness as the Caribbean trade winds push clouds across the blue sky above.

It's beautiful in a raw, untamed way that money can't buy, only stumble across and claim.

And on the screen before me is Scarletta, suspended in that very light.

She's leaned into her challenge with every ounce of herself. She's given me everything—her trust, her fear, her absolute surrender. The completeness of it makes my chest tight with something I don't have adequate words for.

I'm not disappointed that she used her safe word.

Not even remotely.

In fact, I'm intensely, viscerally proud of my good little

slut for having the courage and self-awareness to do so. For trusting me enough to believe I would honor it without question or hesitation.

And the reason she gave—Jesus Christ, the reason. My God. Could there possibly be a better, more perfect reason to invoke that protection?

I want to remember everything.

She was afraid of blacking out. Of losing this experience.

Not losing her *agency*, which would also be valid.

Losing her *experience*.

She wanted to stay present for every moment of what I was giving her.

That's not weakness. That's the opposite of weakness. That's a woman who understands her own psychology well enough to recognize the warning signs, who trusts me enough to believe I'll stop when she asks, and who values our experience together enough to protect it from her own neurological defense mechanisms.

She could have let herself slip away. Could have surrendered to the blackout and woken up afterward with fragmented memories and confusion. Instead, she fought for consciousness. Fought to stay with me.

I replay the moment in my mind—her voice cracking on that single syllable, *red*, the way her body went slack with relief when I immediately powered down the wand and began releasing her restraints. No hesitation. No negotiation. No disappointment in my expression or my touch.

That's what builds trust. Not the scenes themselves, but the moments between them. The proof that her boundaries are sacred.

My thoughts drift forward, constructing the evening ahead with the same precision I bring to everything.

After the maze, I'll have lunch brought to the pavilion overlooking the eastern beach. Nothing elaborate—grilled mahi-mahi, fresh fruit, a light salad. She'll need protein after the physical exertion of the morning, and I want her alert, not sluggish from heavy food.

Thirty minutes to decompress. To let her nervous system settle back toward baseline.

But I won't let her sit across from me like we're colleagues sharing a meal.

No.

I'll make her kneel between my legs on the cushion I've already had placed there. I'll feed her pieces of steak from my fingers, watch her lips close around each morsel. Slices of mango, still cold from the refrigerator, the juice running down her chin until I wipe it away with my thumb.

She'll suck my fingers clean after each bite. Slowly. Deliberately. Maintaining eye contact while her tongue works between my knuckles.

And when I'm finished eating, when she's had enough sustenance to carry her through the afternoon, I'll unzip my trousers and guide her mouth to my cock.

Not to finish. Not yet.

Just to feel her warmth, her submission, her willingness to serve. She'll hold me in her mouth while I stroke her hair and tell her what a good little slut she's being. How proud I am of her performance this morning.

I might fuck her throat, if she's exceptionally good. If she demonstrates the kind of eager surrender that makes my control slip.

But probably not.

That particular reward will wait for later. For after she's truly earned it.

Stations Four and Five are already prepared—both designed purely for dominance and submission without the fear factors that characterized this morning's challenges. No heights. No hunters. No psychological pressure beyond the simple, clarifying dynamic of my control and her obedience.

Just kink. Just connection. Just a gentle wind-down toward evening.

Then the spa.

A smile tugs at the corner of my mouth as I consider what awaits her there.

The attendants will be present, of course. They'll bathe her, massage her, tend to every inch of her exhausted body with professional precision. But their hands will remain clinical tonight. No teasing strokes. No fingers drifting toward her pussy. No orchestrated arousal.

If she's aching—and she will be, I'm absolutely certain of that—she will be denied.

I will not let her orgasm again until tomorrow.

And tonight, in my bed, I will not touch her sexually at all. My hands will remain above her waist, holding her against my chest while she sleeps. My cock will stay in my boxer briefs despite whatever desperate, unconscious movements she makes against me in the night.

Forging bonds.

That's what tonight is for.

Not pleasure, not release… but… *connection.*

The flicker on the left wall of monitors pulls my attention away from Scarletta.

I watch the static ripple across the Chaff Island feed, a momentary distortion that shouldn't be happening. A reminder that I missed a detail.

I clench my jaw, irritation threading through the satisfaction I was feeling moments ago. I should have scheduled maintenance before Volk arrived. Should have had my tech team sweep every camera, every relay station, every backup power source on that island. Instead, I was too focused on perfecting Scarletta's experience, too consumed with the details of her stations to attend to the mundane necessities of Volk's disposal.

Sloppy.

The Station Three security room surrounds me—a climate-controlled concrete bunker built directly into the hillside, connected to the aftercare suite through a reinforced steel door that Scarletta will never see. Every station on Story Island has an identical setup. Sixteen monitors arranged in a four-by-four grid on each wall. Redundant power supplies. Satellite uplink for remote access. Biometric locks that respond only to my fingerprint and retinal scan.

A place to monitor absolutely everything.

A place designed for me to maintain absolute control.

I built this infrastructure over several years, pouring millions into systems that most governments couldn't afford. Because control isn't just about the scenes themselves. It's about knowing. Seeing. Understanding every variable before it becomes a problem.

The Chaff Island feed stabilizes, and I study the image with clinical detachment.

Volk lies face-down in the mud approximately six hundred meters from where he triggered the 'Honeypot' station. He hasn't moved in hours according to the subcutaneous tracking device pulsing data to my secondary monitor. His vitals tell the story his motionless body obscures—respiration shallow but present, heart rate elevated with periodic adrenaline spikes that suggest consciousness, core temperature dropping as the jungle floor leaches heat from his prone form.

The fire ant venom has done its work.

His cardiovascular system is failing, the accumulated toxins overwhelming whatever remained of his physical reserves. Death is most certainly less than an hour away, possibly sooner if his heart gives out before his lungs fill with fluid.

I feel nothing watching him die. No satisfaction, no triumph, no dark pleasure in his suffering. Just the quiet acknowledgment that another predator has been removed from circulation, another monster who will never touch another child.

The Scales balance.

But Volk's cleanup is going to ruin this evening.

The realization settles into my chest with an unpleasant weight. Protocol demands I retrieve the body, transport it to the cremation facility in the cave system, and dispose of every trace. The process requires a minimum of four hours when accounting for boat transit, body handling, and thorough site sanitation.

Four hours away from Scarletta tonight.

Four hours when I could be holding her against my chest in the spa, feeding her dinner on the terrace, watching her eyes grow heavy with exhaustion and contentment as the evening wind carries the scent of jasmine through the open windows.

I just want to enjoy her.

The thought surfaces with surprising intensity, almost petulant in its simplicity. I've spent six months planning this weekend, every detail calibrated for maximum impact, and now a dead trafficker is going to steal hours from my carefully constructed timeline.

I force myself to put Volk aside. That sick bastard isn't going to ruin my plans. I've worked too hard for this day.

The maze has always been one of my favorite stations on Story Island, but it wasn't always configured for this particular fantasy.

Three months ago, the labyrinth was a standard psychological challenge—bamboo walls, disorienting pathways, timed pressure elements designed to push participants toward vulnerability.

Effective enough for the women who came through the auction system seeking controlled fear and carefully negotiated submission.

But then I found *her* story.

I had acquired the DarkDesires forum several months before stumbling onto Scarletta's writing. It was one of dozens of similar platforms I purchased through shell corporations during that period, each acquisition serving a dual purpose.

The forums gave me access to potential submissives worth pursuing, women whose writing revealed psychological depths that vanilla dating sites could never expose.

And… they gave me *targets*.

Men who posted too eagerly about ignoring boundaries, about pushing past resistance, about the thrill of taking what wasn't offered.

The Scales needed fresh prey.

And I needed something else entirely.

There was a darkness brewing inside me during those months that had nothing to do with justice or retribution. A yearning for something I couldn't quite name.

An evil, maybe. Brewing inside me. I wanted to punish more than just the obvious billionaire. I wanted my justice to reach the 'common man' too. For the truly sick and twisted exist on every economic level.

Scarletta was the first writer on DarkDesires who made me stop scrolling.

Her prose was sharp, psychologically sophisticated, and unflinching in its examination of power dynamics. Where other writers dressed up their fantasies in flowery language and romantic justifications, Scarletta wrote with surgical precision about the mechanics of surrender.

About the shame that fueled desire.

About protagonists who craved darkness not despite their intelligence, but because of it.

I read everything she'd posted within a week of discovering her account. Then I read it again… and again… and again.

The cameras went up in her apartment almost immediately.

Looking back now, the timing was something of a lucky break. Scarletta almost never leaves her studio—days can pass without her stepping outside, her entire existence compressed into four hundred square feet of unwashed dishes, blanket forts, and the blue glow of her laptop screen.

But that particular week, she was earnestly trying to find a job. A desperate attempt to address the financial situation that was already spiraling toward the eviction notice I would eventually exploit.

She left every day for at least four hours, trudging through Idaho Falls in her best clothes, going on interviews to coffee shops and bookstores that would never call her back.

My team installed sixteen cameras and a keystroke logger while she was gone.

That night, I found the folder labeled 'DO NOT OPEN.'

The Call of the Labyrinth.

I knew from the first paragraph that this was different from everything else she'd written. Darker. More dangerous.

His clawed hand wraps around my throat. I know I should fight. Should scream. Should do anything except what my body is doing right now, which is melting into his grip like I've been waiting my entire life for exactly this pressure against my pulse.

"You ran so beautifully," he growls, his voice resonating through my chest. "But you were never going to escape. You were always going to end up here. Underneath me. Begging for the monster you pretended to fear."

I want to deny it. Want to spit in his face to prove I still have a shred of dignity left after everything the maze took from me.

But it's a lie. So instead, I whisper… "Please."

He smiles at me with too many long, sharp teeth. "Please what, little runner?"

"Please ruin me."

So he does.

His cock is inhuman—thick, and ridged, and far too large for my body to accommodate. But my body doesn't care about accommodation. My body opens for him like it's been designed for this exact violation, stretching around his impossible girth while I scream, and sob, and beg him never to stop.

"You're mine now," he snarls this into my ear as he bottoms out inside me, his claws drawing blood from my hips. "Every part of you. Every thought. Every breath. Every orgasm. Mine."

I come so hard, the darkness obliterates my sight. Sends me into a state of unconscious oblivion.

When I wake, he's still inside me, still moving, and I realize with devastating clarity that I don't want to escape anymore.

I want to stay in his animalistic darkness forever.

The story breaks every consent law, both real and implied.

In the legal world, what Helix does to Lyra constitutes kidnapping, assault, and rape.

In the book world—even in the darkest corners of erotic fiction where consent can be negotiated and fantasized—the story crosses lines that most platforms *explicitly* forbid.

Obviously, Scarletta figured this out early because she never put it online. She hid it away in that folder, a shameful secret she couldn't delete but couldn't share, a fantasy too dark even for her anonymous ScarletSins persona.

I jerked off to that story twice a day for two months straight.

I could not get it out of my mind.

The beastly nature of Helix, his absolute certainty that Lyra belonged to him. How much bigger he was than her, how he filled her so completely that there was no room left for anything except him. How Lyra ran from it, fought it, and then took it and loved it with a desperation that made my hand move faster on my cock every single time.

God, I was obsessed.

Looking back, I recognize that I was out of control during that period.

The surveillance escalated beyond anything I'd done with previous targets. The fantasies grew more elaborate, more consuming, bleeding into my waking hours until I could barely focus on MacLeay Capital, or The Scales, or anything that wasn't Scarletta's face on my monitors, Scarletta's words on my screen, Scarletta's soft moans when she touched herself to her own stories without knowing I was watching.

That's what really spurred the whole Derek situation.

I was just… *out of control.*

When I discovered what he'd done to her—reading her frantic, tearful journal entries through her hacked hard drive, watching her curl into a ball on her bed and sob for hours—something in me snapped with an almost audible crack.

The methodical patience I usually brought to Scales operations evaporated entirely. I tracked Derek down within seventy-two hours, and what I did to him had nothing to do with justice, or balance, or making the world safer for innocents.

It was personal.

It was emotional.

It was the most satisfying kill I've ever made.

I've dialed it back since then—forced myself to regain the control that defines everything I am, everything I've built.

But only because I found a healthier outlet for the obsession.

I recreated the Helix maze here, on Story Island.

The construction took three months and cost more than most people's houses. Custom bamboo walls grown to specification. Portal archways with concealed and nearly silent hydraulics that create the illusion of teleportation. A wireless sound system and custom earbuds to replicate the way Scarletta described Helix's telepathy in Lyra's head.

And the costumes.

Fuck, the costumes for my attendants are out of this world good.

Horns. Claws. Voice modulators that transform human speech into something inhuman and predatory. Every detail pulled directly from her manuscript, recreated with obsessive precision because I need her to believe she's stepped inside her own death-spiral imagination.

The maze has been ready for five weeks now.

And I've been planning to put my good little slut inside it since the day the final camera was installed.

I lean in, almost pressing my nose to the screen as Scarletta comes into view on the monitor. She's approaching the entrance…

CHAPTER 14
SCARLETTA

The maze entrance rises before me like something that shouldn't exist outside my own head.

Bamboo walls stretch fifteen feet high, woven so tightly I can't see through them, can't cheat by glimpsing what waits inside. The archway is exactly how I described it in the story —rough-hewn wood covered in carved symbols that look ancient and vaguely threatening.

He built this.

The thought won't settle properly in my brain.

He read my unpublished nightmare fantasy and built it into physical reality.

I stop walking. The earth below my feet is smooth, powdery, and deep. Like here, on this island, even the dirt is controlled by the unmasked man's obsessions.

Torches flicker in iron sconces on either side of the entrance, casting dancing shadows across the bamboo. The air smells like smoke, and jungle rot, and citronella—reminding me that this isn't real. This is theatre.

Very expensive theater.

Insanely expensive theater.

For me.

The archway seems to breathe in the firelight, and I notice speakers hidden in the carved wood, positioned exactly where I imagined Helix's telepathic voice would originate from. A small basket sits on a pedestal just inside the entrance, containing what looks like wireless earbuds.

My pussy clenches at the sight of them.

He's going to be inside my head.

The Call of the Labyrinth comes back to me like an old friend…

I stumble, falling. My chest hits the hard dirt and the air flows out of me in a loud breath. For a moment, I can't breathe. I just lie there, unsure what just happened. The claws, the teeth, the horns!

He was a monster!

Touching me, groping me!

His fingers between my legs and… oh, God.

The throbbing is back. the wetness pouring out of me like —

Trees rustle somewhere behind me.

I shake myself out of the ridiculous fantasy inside my sick head, pull myself up, and find… a maze?

What the fuck! I want to screams this, but I don't dare. He'll hear me. Capture me.

And then what will he do, Lyra?

Fuck me…

Stop it! You're a sick piece of shit! It's not even human! It's an animal walking on two legs, nothing more!

And he's going to rape you if you don't snap the fuck out of what's happening here and pull yourself together!

I push the panic and arousal down and force myself to focus. The maze entrance rises in front of me like a mouth waiting to swallow me whole.

Behind me, the monster approaches. His footsteps are wrong and heavy. He's not running. He doesn't need to run. He knows exactly where I am.

I look up at the carved archway, at the symbols I don't under-

stand, and I realize I don't know where I am. I get to my feet, spin-
ning around, desperate to understand

"Little Lyra." His voice echoes through the trees, through my
skull, through my bones. "Did you think I'd let you go?"

Blinking, I snap out of the scene. A scene that's so familiar, even four years after writing it, I know all the words. Every detail, every turn of the maze, every plant, every monster waiting inside.

It was… my first sick fantasy.

The first sign of my disgusting perversion.

Letting out a breath, I look over my shoulder.

The jungle path behind me is empty. No footsteps. No monster.

It's not sick.

Not like this.

It's just… fun. That's all. It's fun. Safe, consensual, dirty—I smile a little. Because it is *definitely* dirty.

But it's a fantasy I had.

Have.

Still have.

And I want to live it.

I don't care what that says about me, I want to live it.

I know the rules of the maze. I wrote them.

Three monsters hunt the labyrinth. If one catches you, they claim you.

And by claim, I mean grope, finger, fuck. Whatever they want.

Lyra gets caught by each of them. Is violated each time, and comes each time. Her arousal a betrayal of her body. But she enjoys it. I know this because I wrote her.

Am… her.

The unmasked man already let it slip that the monsters are the attendants. I'm sure they'll be scary—wearing costumes. But they've already proved they can easily arouse me.

I'm going to enjoy that to the fullest. I can't wait to be caught.

It's probably just as wrong to enjoy this attendant gang-bang as it was to write a whole story about a girl who wants to be raped by monsters, but… whatever.

Helix is in the maze too, and I assume that part is being played by the unmasked man. The center holds a portal that promises escape. The portal is a lie.

In my story, Lyra learned this the hard way.

I step toward the pedestal and lift the basket with trembling fingers. Inside are two wireless earbuds and a strip of silk the color of dried blood.

A blindfold.

In the story, Lyra wasn't blindfolded. She was *blinded*—a plant squirted purple powder into her face the moment she entered. Temporary. Terrifying. She stumbled through the first quarter of the maze with her eyes burning and useless, guided only by the monster's voice in her skull as he 'helped' her try to outrun the monsters.

Of course, this was also a lie.

Helix wanted to *watch* Lyra be caught. He wanted to watch her struggle. He wanted to see if she could take their cocks, their claws, their teeth.

Because every one of those things on *him*, was going to be worse.

Am I scared?

Slightly. But in a good way.

In the end, I'm going to get what I came for.

My deepest, darkest desire made real.

I pick up the blindfold, holding it in my hands as I notice a rope anchored to the right side of the entrance, thick and rough, disappearing into the maze at waist height. A small card hangs from it on a string:

If you get lost, follow the rope. It will take care of you.

Take care of me.

What does that mean?

Does it lead to the center? To him? To one of the monsters?

There's no way to know.

I'm smiling when I put the ear buds in and they come to life with the sound of heavy breathing. Wet and throbbing when I tie the blind fold on.

The breathing fills my skull, like something alive pressed against my ear from the inside.

Then the whisper comes.

"Welcome, my little slut."

My pussy clenches so hard my knees nearly buckle.

"You are about to have the experience of a lifetime."

His voice is everywhere. Inside me. Around me. The earbuds seal out the jungle sounds completely—no birds, no wind, no rustling leaves.

Just him.

"When you're ready, take eight steps forward."

Eight steps.

Eight steps.

In the story, Lyra took eight steps before the purple powder blinded her. Eight steps into the mouth of the maze before she lost her sight and had to trust the monster's voice to guide her.

I'm already blind.

Already trusting.

I take the first step, and the powdery earth shifts under my bare foot like it's been waiting for me.

One.

"That's it, little slut. Keep walking for me."

Two.

"Do you know what I'm going to do to you when I catch you?"

Three.

"I'm going to spread you open on the altar at the center of this maze."

Four.

"I'm going to make you beg for my cock while you're still crying from what my monsters did to you."

Five.

"I'm going to fuck every hole you have until you forget your own name."

Six.

"Until the only word left in that pretty head is *Master*."

Seven.

My breathing is ragged now, each inhale catching in my throat like a sob. The blindfold presses against my closed eyes. The darkness is absolute. The voice is *everything*.

"Until you understand that you were *made* to be mine."

Eight.

I stop.

The air feels different here. Heavier. The bamboo walls must be close on either side—I can sense them even without seeing, the way the sound of my own breathing changes in the enclosed space.

"Good girl."

The praise hits my clit like a physical touch.

"But before you can become mine, you must prove yourself worthy."

Worthy.

The word echoes through four years of shame and longing and desperate late-night writing sessions. The word I gave to Helix. The word I made Lyra earn through blood, and come, and terror.

My whole body is trembling.

"Ready, little slut?"

I nod, even though he can't see me. Even though maybe he can. Even though I don't know anything anymore except that I want this.

I *need* this.

The silence stretches for one heartbeat. Two.

Then he screams it:

"RUN, LITTLE SLUT! FIFTEEN STRIDES!"

A growl explodes through the earbuds—guttural, inhuman, *close*—and I'm running before my brain catches up to my legs, counting strides through the darkness, heart slamming against my ribs, the monster's snarl chasing me through my skull.

I run.

Not the clumsy, terrified scramble I expected—something else. Something that feels like flying through darkness, my feet finding the powdery earth with impossible certainty.

My brain is counting, but my body already knows. Already remembers.

The walls brush my shoulders—I *feel* them, the rough bamboo catching briefly on my skin as I squeeze through. Exactly how I wrote it. Exactly how Lyra did it.

"Ten strides left, little slut."

His voice fills my skull, but I'm already adjusting my trajectory. Already angling left for the gentle curve that leads to the second corridor.

He replicated it.

He fucking *replicated* it.

Every measurement. Every turn. Every goddamn stride count from a story I wrote.

Seven. Eight. Nine.

The growling in my ears shifts. Hungrier. Wetter. Snarling like it wants to eat me.

Ten.

Something sharp catches my hip just as the masked man's voice yells, "Five strides right!"

I gasp—a high, startled sound that doesn't feel like it belongs to me—and my stride falters. The sting is immediate, bright, real. Not theatrical. Not pretend.

Blood. I can feel it. A thin line of warmth sliding down my thigh.

It cut me.

A claw. An actual fucking claw.

Of course it cut you, Scarletta. This is Max Fear Factor. This is the real deal. This is—

Thirteen.

Shit! I was supposed to turn!

I just keep running, desperately trying to map the maze in my head as, again, something snags my skin!

My thigh this time. I scream, it *hurts!*

What the fuck!

The first capture doesn't happen until—

I slip on something—mud! Why is it muddy? There's no mud! A moment later, I'm on the ground, face first. Dirt in my teeth.

The snarling in my ears is so loud, the fall so unexpected, the pain in my hip so real—I... *I can't do this!*

I rip the blindfold off, and find... *nothing.*

Nothing behind me. Nothing in front of me.

It's just me in this mud and... I look down.

My brain stutters for a moment. Because there's something wrong with it. Something very, very *wrong* with it.

It looks like... blood.

I look at my hip, my thigh—blood is flowing out. It's trickling down both sides of my leg.

But... it's a trickle and the blood underneath me is... a puddle.

Slowly, I turn my head.

And I scream...

Because on the ground, in his own puddle of blood, is the face of the blonde attendant, blue eyes open, his body... no where to be found.

I scream—a raw, throat-tearing sound that echoes through the maze—and in the exact same heartbeat, I register movement behind me. Too close. Too fast.

Before I can even think to scramble away, thick fingers

tangle violently in my hair, yanking hard enough that white spots burst across my vision. The pain is instant and electric, radiating from my scalp down my spine.

Then I'm being dragged.

I'm hauled backward like a sack, my heels scraping uselessly against the earth as whoever has me pulls me down the narrow path. My fingers claw at the ground, trying to find purchase, trying to stop this, but there's nothing to grab onto except slick mud and the rough edge of bamboo that tears at my palms.

"This isn't how it happens!" I scream, my voice cracking with hysteria. The words tear out of me, desperate, pleading. "This isn't how it goes! *Red!*" I shriek it like a prayer, like an incantation that might somehow undo whatever nightmare I've stumbled into. "*Red, red, red!*"

My captor's response is immediate and brutal—a bare foot slams into my ribs, knocking the air from my lungs in a painful whoosh. The impact sends me rolling sideways into the mud, and for a second all I can do is gasp like a fish on land, trying to remember how to breathe.

When I finally manage to drag my eyes upward, squinting through the pain and the film of tears blurring my vision, I see him properly for the first time.

And he's *wrong*.

This man—this person looming over me with one mud-caked foot still raised—is someone I have never seen before.

Not one of the three masked attendants I was expecting. Not anyone from Caleb's carefully constructed fantasy.

He's older, maybe in his fifties, with a weathered face that speaks of years lived hard. His skin is smeared with thick mud that's dried in patches, flaking off in places to reveal pale flesh underneath. But it's not just mud covering him. There's something else—something dark and sticky coating his arms, his chest, glistening wetly in the dappled light filtering through the bamboo.

"Who... who the *fuck* are you?" The words tear out of me in a ragged scream that doesn't even sound like my own voice anymore.

His face is caked in so much filth I can barely make out his features—just those pale blue eyes blazing out from beneath the grime, utterly devoid of anything human. Cold. Predatory. *Evil.*

When he speaks, it comes out as a guttural growl, harsh syllables that scrape against my ears like broken glass. I don't understand a single word, but the cadence, the harsh consonants—they sound suspiciously like... Russian?

My brain short-circuits trying to process this. Russian. *Russian.* What the actual fuck is happening? This wasn't part of the script. This wasn't part of any of it.

"*Red!*" I scream again, my voice pitching higher. "Red, red, *red!*"

CHAPTER 15
CALEB

I strip off my shirt, tossing it onto the chair beside the console. My pants follow. I'm already half-hard thinking about what comes next—Scarletta navigating the maze blindfolded, my voice in her ear, the hunt playing out exactly as she wrote it.

Three months of planning. Every bamboo wall measured to match her manuscript. Every portal archway calibrated to disorient her in precisely the ways she described. The monster costumes cost forty thousand dollars each, custom-fabricated prosthetics that would make Hollywood jealous.

My boxer briefs come off, my hand going to my cock automatically.

How I will fuck this girl today.

What she got from me so far… it's nothing compared to how I'll take her in the center of the maze. I picture her on her knees, my cock buried in her mouth, The tip pressing against the back of her throat—

A scream cuts through the monitors.

I turn, frowning. She's barely started. The first capture isn't supposed to happen for another eight minutes minimum, and even then, the attendants know to build the tension slowly, to let her hear them before they touch her.

This scream is wrong—pitched too high, ragged with genuine terror rather than the delicious fear we've been cultivating all day.

My eyes find her feed, and my brain simply stops.

The image doesn't make sense.

I stare at it, waiting for the visual to resolve into something rational, something that fits within the parameters of what should be happening on my island.

There's a man in the maze.

A man who is *not* one of my attendants.

The build is wrong, the posture is wrong, everything is wrong. He's covered in mud, caked with it, and he's dragging Scarletta by her hair through the dirt while she screams.

"Red! Red!"

Her voice tears through the speakers, and the word hits me like a physical blow. She's safewording. She's actually safewording, and the man—whoever the fuck he is—doesn't stop.

He kicks her. He *kicks her* in the ribs and she crumples, and I watch her mouth form the word again, desperate, pleading.

Time dilates into something thick and syrupy.

The cameras. The glitches I dismissed. The digital artifacts and blur on the Chaff Island feeds that I attributed to humidity and scheduled for maintenance.

My head snaps to the secondary wall of monitors. Volk's feed. The body is still there, face-down in the mud, covered in fire ants exactly as it should be.

Except.

The body hasn't moved in hours. Not a twitch. Not a single involuntary spasm from the venom coursing through his system. I'd noticed it earlier and assumed he was dead or dying, but now—

I zoom in on the Chaff Island feed, and the image stutters. Pixelates. Reforms.

The resolution is wrong. The shadows don't match the

current position of the sun. The timestamp in the corner reads correctly, but the light filtering through the jungle canopy is at least two hours off from where it should be.

Loop.

Someone looped my fucking cameras.

My gaze returns to the maze feed, to the mud-covered man with pale eyes who has my Scarletta by the throat now, and the pieces click together with the precision of a closing trap.

Dimitri Volkov isn't dead in the jungle.

Dimitri Volkov is in my maze.

Time snaps back into focus.

I'm moving before my conscious mind finishes processing. The control room door crashes open and I'm sprinting through the jungle, my bare feet hitting roots and rocks and I don't feel any of it. The undergrowth tears at my legs. I'm naked. I'm fucking *naked* and unarmed and Scarletta is in there with a man who has spent fifteen years trafficking children, a man who knows exactly what happens to people who cross me, a man with nothing left to lose.

The maze entrance looms ahead. I designed every inch of this labyrinth. I know the optimal paths, the portal archways, the dead ends. I can reach the center in four minutes if I run the correct route.

I round the first corner at full speed.

A body lies crumpled against the bamboo wall.

The monster costume is still mostly intact—the elaborate prosthetic clawed gloves, the voice modulator hanging loose around what remains of his neck. But his head is gone.

A scream rips through the air behind me. Female. High-pitched. Not Scarletta—the timbre is wrong, the accent different. It's coming from the direction of the preparation pavilion, at least half a mile back.

Another scream answers it. Male this time. Deeper in the jungle, toward the eastern shore.

The sounds multiply, overlapping, a chorus of terror spreading across my island like wildfire.

How long?

The question burns through my skull as I vault over the headless body and sprint deeper into the maze.

How long has Volk been free?

The camera loop was sophisticated. Professional. Not something he could have improvised from inside a cage on Chaff Island. Someone helped him. Someone with access to my security infrastructure, someone who knew the camera protocols well enough to insert a seamless recording without triggering my redundancy alerts.

I mentally calculate the timeline. The glitches started approximately six hours ago. I noticed them, dismissed them, moved on. Six hours is enough time to swim the channel between islands if you're desperate and strong.

Another scream, this one truncated sharply into silence.

I run faster, my lungs burning, my mind racing through the implications. Volk didn't just escape. He planned this. He had inside help. He turned my hunt into his hunt, and now he's loose on an island full of staff and attendants who weren't prepared for a predator.

But none of that matters.

None of it matters because Scarletta is somewhere in this maze with him, and every second I spend calculating is a second he has his hands on her.

I hit the first portal archway and don't hesitate, plunging through into the disorienting darkness that deposits me thirty yards deeper into the labyrinth.

The mud here is churned, disturbed. Fresh drag marks cut through it like wounds.

I follow the trail.

I plunge through the second portal, the disorientation lasting only a heartbeat before my feet hit solid ground. The maze walls blur past as I sprint, my mental map updating in real-time—two turns left, then the center opens up.

Scarletta's screams have changed.

They're wild now. Primal. The kind of sound that comes from somewhere deeper than fear, somewhere that touches madness. Each one drives into my chest like a blade, and I push harder, my legs burning, my lungs on fire.

I round the first turn.

Her screams fracture into something worse—a keening wail that rises and falls, rises and falls, the rhythm of someone watching horror unfold and being unable to stop it.

Second turn.

The bamboo walls fall away and the center platform spreads before me, exactly as I designed it—the circular clearing, the raised platform covered in banana leaves, the ground-level eye bolts for restraints.

Scarletta is on her knees in the mud.

She's covered in blood.

My heart stops. Actually stops. The muscle seizes in my chest and for one infinite second, I am nothing but frozen terror, staring at the red coating her skin, her hair, her face. So much red. Too much red. The color of arterial spray, of opened arteries, of death.

Then my eyes process what they're seeing.

The blood isn't hers.

It's splattered across her in patterns that don't match wounds—cast-off from something else, from *someone* else. The dark-haired attendant lies three feet from her, his throat opened in a ragged smile, his chest still twitching with the last electrical impulses of a dying nervous system.

Volk stands over him, a hunting knife in his hand, and when he sees me, he *smiles*.

He spits on Scarletta. A thick glob of phlegm lands in her hair, and she flinches, her wild screams dying into hitching sobs.

Then he looks up and points at the sky, shouting something in Russian.

I hear it now. The distant thrum of rotor blades cutting through air, growing louder.

A helicopter.

He's being rescued.

The pieces fall into place with sickening clarity. The insider help. The looped cameras. The access codes. Someone arranged extraction, someone with resources and reach, someone who knew exactly when and how to pull Volk off this island before I could finish what I started.

Volk's smile widens. He thinks he's won. He thinks that helicopter changes the equation, tips the scales back in his favor, gives him leverage.

Oh, hell the fuck no.

The rage doesn't hit me like a wave. It settles into my bones like ice water, cold, and clear, and absolutely still. My heartbeat slows. My breathing evens out. The world narrows to this moment, this clearing, this man.

I begin to circle.

Volk tracks me, the knife held loose in his grip, professional. He's killed before. Probably many times. But he's killed the weak, the helpless, the children he trafficked and the witnesses he silenced.

He's never faced something like me.

The helicopter grows louder, but I calculate distances automatically. The only viable landing zone is the runway near the preparation pavilion—nearly a mile through dense jungle. Even at a dead sprint, whoever's on that aircraft won't reach us for at least twelve minutes.

This will be over in three.

I keep circling, and when I speak, I speak in Russian. His mother tongue. The language of his nightmares.

"*Ty dumal, chto uydyosh', Dimitri?*" The words slide out

smooth as silk. My Russian is perfect. *"I'll tear out your heart and make you watch me eat it."*

His smile flickers.

I continue in Russian. *"First I'll cut off your balls. Slowly. With a dull knife. Then I'll shove them down your throat and watch you choke."*

I keep moving, a slow orbit that forces him to turn, to track me, to take his eyes off Scarletta for seconds at a time.

"You trafficked children for fifteen years. I know every name. Every face. When I'm done with you, they'll only find pieces."

Volk's jaw tightens. The knife shifts in his grip.

"Your sister's still alive, yes? In Moscow?" I let the words hang between us like a blade. *"After I send her your head, I'll visit her. And I will make her balance your scale. Because nothing I do to you now, will ever be enough to erase the sin of touching her."*

I nod my head at Scarletta, cowering in fear and covered in blood in the dirt.

Volk lunges, and the world slows to crystalline clarity.

His knife hand arcs toward my throat—standard prison-yard slash, predictable and desperate.

I pivot left, letting the blade whisper past my carotid by less than an inch, and my right hand closes around his wrist like a vise.

The joint doesn't break cleanly. I feel the tendons stretch, the ligaments tear, the small bones grinding against each other as I twist. The sound is wet, organic, deeply satisfying.

The knife drops into the mud.

Volk screams.

I'm hard.

Rock fucking hard.

My cock swinging heavy between my thighs as I drive my knee into his solar plexus. The air leaves his lungs in a whoosh and he doubles over, and I bring my elbow down on the back of his skull with enough force to split skin.

Blood.

His blood this time.

It sprays across my chest, hot and copper-bright, and my erection throbs in response.

This is what I am.

This is what I've always been.

The mask of civilization, the suits, and board meetings, and calculated charm—all of it falls away when I'm doing what I was born to do.

Volk tries to rally. Credit where it's due—the man survived for thirty years in the trafficking underworld, eliminated witnesses, evaded every law enforcement agency on three continents. He knows how to fight dirty.

His thumb goes for my eye socket.

I catch his hand and break two fingers, the bones snapping like dry twigs. Then I break two more. His screams echo off the bamboo walls, beautiful and raw, and Scarletta is sobbing somewhere behind me but I can't focus on that right now.

Can't focus on anything but this.

I drag Volk to the center platform, to the eye bolts I installed for restraining Scarletta. The irony isn't lost on me.

My cock bobs against my thigh with every step, flushed and leaking, and I don't care.

Don't care that she's watching.

Don't care about the helicopter getting closer.

Don't care about anything except making this last.

"You thought the children would forget?" I hiss in his ear as I force him face-down onto the platform.

I secure his wrists to the bolts with the leather cuffs meant for my little writer. They're too tight, but it doesn't matter. He's not going to need circulating blood for much longer.

The hunting knife lies in the mud where he dropped it. I retrieve it, test the edge against my thumb. Sharp enough. Barely.

A dull knife will hurt more.

I start with his Achilles tendons. The blade saws through

the first one with a wet, gristly resistance, and Volk's scream tears through the jungle, scattering birds from the canopy above. His legs spasm uselessly, feet flopping at wrong angles, and my cock twitches in response.

The second tendon takes longer. I go slower deliberately, feeling every fiber part beneath the blade, watching his body arch against the restraints in agony.

"Five hundred and fifty-three children." I tell him, still in Russian, as I move to kneel beside his prone body. *"That's how many we confirmed. How many were there really, Dimitri?"*

He's crying now. Sobbing in Russian, begging in Russian, promising money, connections, information. The usual currency of the desperate.

I don't want any of it.

I want his suffering.

The knife traces down his spine, not cutting, just promising. His back muscles clench and release, clench and release. I'm so hard it hurts, pre-come dripping onto the platform beside his hip, and the sight of it makes me groan.

"I'm going to cut out your heart. But not yet."

I begin with his fingers. The ones that signed trafficking orders. The ones that touched children. I take them off at the first knuckle—index, middle, ring, pinky—and his screams blend into one continuous howl of agony.

Somewhere distant, a woman is crying. Scarletta. I should check on her. I should comfort her. I should be the protector she needs.

But the knife is in my hand, and Volk's blood is warm on my skin, and my cock is so fucking hard I can barely think.

I move to his other hand.

Thumb first this time. The bone crunches under the dull blade, requires sawing, requires *effort*, and Volk's voice breaks into something beyond screaming—a high, thin keen that sounds almost inhuman.

Beautiful.

More fingers fall. The severed digits scattered across the platform like obscene confetti. Blood pools beneath him, black in the jungle shadows, and I stroke myself once, twice, unable to resist.

The helicopter noise has faded. Or maybe I've stopped hearing it. The world has narrowed to this platform, this body, this righteous act of destruction.

"Time for castration."

I release the wrist restraints and roll him onto his back. His face is gray, shock setting in, but his eyes are still aware. Still terrified.

Good. I want him conscious for this part.

His cock is shriveled, his balls contracted. Fear has made them small.

The blade presses against the base of his scrotum.

"Пожалуйста." *Please.*

I cut.

The sound he makes isn't human. It's something primal, something that comes from the deepest part of the brainstem where language doesn't exist. His body convulses so violently the blood fountains from his groin, arterial spray painting my chest and stomach crimson.

My hand finds my cock again. I'm stroking in earnest now, slicked with his blood, and it's wrong, so fucking wrong, but I can't stop.

Don't want to stop.

This is who I am.

His screaming has dissolved into wet gurgling. I've nicked the femoral artery—he'll bleed out within minutes if I don't cauterize. I could save him. Prolong this.

I choose not to.

Instead, I watch his eyes dim as I jerk myself faster, harder, my balls drawing tight against my body. His mouth moves soundlessly. Prayers, maybe. Curses. It doesn't matter.

His last breath rattles out just as my orgasm hits—a

violent, full-body shudder that tears a groan from my throat. I come across his chest, across the ruin I've made of him, rope after rope of come mixing with his cooling blood.

The release empties me.

I kneel there, panting, my softening cock still in my blood-slicked hand, staring at what I've created.

Justice.

This is justice.

The jungle gradually reasserts itself. Bird calls. Insect hum. The distant thrum of a helicopter that seems to be circling rather than landing.

And behind me, barely audible over the ambient noise—

Crying.

CHAPTER 16
SCARLETTA

Blood.

There's blood on his chest. On his hands. On his—

Don't look at that. Don't look at that. Don't look at—

I look.

The thing on the platform doesn't look like a person anymore. It's pieces. Red pieces, and wet sounds, and the smell of copper and something worse, something organic and wrong, and my brain keeps trying to file it somewhere it can make sense.

He was a bad man. He hurt children. Five hundred and fifty-three children.

The number loops through my head like a broken record.

Five hundred and fifty-three.

Five hundred and fifty-three.

Five hundred and—

The unmasked man is coming toward me. His cock is soft now, blood-streaked, still visible, and I watched him—I watched him *come* while he—

He was protecting you. He saved you. The bad man was going to hurt you and he stopped him.

My brain scrambles for the narrative that makes this

make sense. The one where the hero rescues the maiden, and the villain dies, and everything is justified, and clean, and *right*.

But there's nothing clean about what I just watched.

"Scarletta." His voice cuts through the static. "Scarletta, look at me. Are you hurt? Where did he cut you?"

Hands on my face. Warm. Gentle. The same hands that just—

Don't think about it.

"Your hip. There's blood. Let me see."

I can't speak. My mouth opens but nothing comes out except a sound that might be a sob or might be a scream that got stuck halfway up my throat.

"I need to get you out of here. Can you walk?"

I don't know. I don't know anything. The blonde attendant's head is still there, somewhere behind me in the mud, and the unmasked man is lifting me now, carrying me like I weigh nothing, and his skin is slick with—

Don't.

Don't think about it.

He saved you.

The jungle blurs past. Trees, and vines, and shadows. And I'm shaking so hard my teeth are chattering even though the air is warm and humid. The unmasked man is talking, asking questions I can't process, his voice tight with something that might be concern, or maybe fear.

He came while he was killing him.

The thought surfaces before I can stop it.

He was aroused. He was—

"Stay with me, Scarletta. We're almost there."

The staging pavilion appears through the trees, and there's screaming. More screaming. People in white running, crying, and bodies—

More bodies.

Two staff members on the ground near the entrance, blood

pooling beneath them, and the unmasked man's arms tighten around me as he steps over them.

"Fucking hell," he breathes. "Geoffrey! For fuck's sake... *status report!*"

Someone answers. I don't hear what they say. The world has gone cottony and distant, like I'm watching everything through a screen, like this is footage I'm reviewing rather than something happening to my actual body.

He carries me past the chaos, through a door and into a room. An office. He sets me down on a couch that's too soft, too comfortable, and then he's pressing a glass of water into my hands.

"Drink."

I drink. The water tastes like nothing.

"You're in shock. That's normal. You're safe now."

Safe.

The word doesn't mean anything anymore.

He's pressing something against my hip—gauze, maybe, or a towel—and the sting of it makes me gasp, which is the first sound I've made since the maze.

"Superficial," he says. "Won't even need stitches."

His hands are still bloody. He's leaving red smears on my skin, on the white gauze, on everything he touches.

"Eat something." He pushes a bowl of fruit toward me. Strawberries. Grapes. Normal things that belong to a normal world that doesn't exist anymore.

I stare at them.

"Scarletta. I need you to eat. Your blood sugar—"

I put a grape in my mouth. Chew. Swallow. The motions are mechanical, disconnected from anything like hunger or taste.

He pulls me against his chest, and I should recoil, should fight, should *run*, but instead I just—

Drift.

His heartbeat is steady. Calm.

Like he didn't just torture a man to death.

Like his hands aren't still tacky with blood. Like everything is fine.

Maybe everything *is* fine.

Maybe this is what fine looks like now.

"I have to go manage this." His voice is soft against my hair. "There are protocols to follow. I'll be back as soon as I can."

He eases me down onto the couch, tucks a blanket around me like I'm something precious, something breakable.

"Stay here. Don't open the door for anyone except me."

The lock clicks behind him.

I stare at the ceiling and see nothing but dead bodies and floating heads…

Arms.

Arms around me and I'm screaming before I'm awake, thrashing against something solid and warm that won't let go.

"Hey. Hey. It's me. You're safe."

His voice. The unmasked man's voice.

I blink and the office swims into focus. The couch. The blanket tangled around my legs. The bowl of fruit untouched on the table.

When did I fall asleep?

"Everything's okay." He's lifting me, cradling me against his chest like I weigh nothing. "Everything's fine. I'm going to give you a bath."

Fine.

Fine.

The word bounces around my skull like a marble in a tin can, keeping perfect, metronomic rhythm with the constant, pulsing thump that now fills every available crevice of my brain. Pushing out everything else, leaving behind just that single syllable on endless repeat.

Fine fine fine fine fine.

We're moving. Hallway. Doors. His footsteps steady on tile, then wood, then tile again. He's talking, his voice a low murmur against the top of my head.

"—my private quarters. No one comes in here without permission. You're safe. I've got you."

Safe.

The bamboo walls rise around us.

No.

No.

That's not right. These are concrete walls. White. Clean. But I see the bamboo anyway, see the maze twisting ahead of me, hear Helix's voice in my earbuds telling me to *run, little slut, run.*

"Scarletta?"

The blonde attendant's head in the mud. Eyes open. Mouth slack.

That wasn't in the story. Lyra never found bodies. The monsters in my story didn't—

"You're dissociating. That's normal. Stay with me."

Steam. Warm air on my face. The sound of water running.

I blink and we're in a bathroom. Massive. Marble. A tub the size of a small pool filling with water that smells like lavender.

The bathing pavilion. The stirrups. The blond attendants hands between my—

No. Different room. Different water.

"I'm going to set you down now."

My feet touch cold tile. My knees buckle immediately and he catches me, holds me upright.

"Easy. I've got you."

Helix caught Lyra in the third corridor. Pinned her against the wall. His claws—

The stranger's claws cutting my hip. Real blood. My blood.

That wasn't supposed to happen. In my story, the monsters only made her feel good—

Good, Scarletta? They raped her.

But... she wanted it!

She wanted it?

Even my damaged mind hears myself. Understands what I'm saying. Comprehends just how fucking wrong this is.

"Scarletta. Look at me."

I look.

His face. Handsome. Concerned.

He came while he was killing him.

"You're safe," he says again.

I don't know what that word means anymore.

I don't know what any of this means anymore. I'm not safe. I thought I was. I walked that plank. But I saw the net. I jumped off the platform and did the zip line. But I was wearing the harness.

It *was* safe.

And then... it wasn't.

The water is warm.

That's the first thing that registers—warmth, seeping into muscles I didn't realize were clenched. He lowers me into the tub slowly and carefully.

I drift, detached, disconnected from myself. My thoughts scatter and reform, scatter and reform. Fragments of sensation that won't coalesce into coherent meaning.

The hot water.

His gentle hands.

Violence I can't quite reconcile with this tenderness.

My mind feels afloat. Drifting somewhere above my body, refusing to fully inhabit this moment. Like I'm watching myself from a great distance—a girl in a bathtub being washed by a man whose hands cut the fingers off a bad man.

The contradiction should mean something. Should provoke some response. But I can't hold onto thoughts long enough to examine them. They slip away before I can grasp their edges, leaving only this strange, cottony emptiness where my reactions should be.

He's washing me now. Gentle strokes with a soft cloth, starting at my shoulders, working down my arms.

His voice washes over me like the water. Meaningless sounds arranged in meaningless patterns. Small talk. He's making *small talk* while he cleans the blood off my skin.

The cloth moves across my collarbone. Down my sternum. Gentle circles on my stomach.

He sighs.

The sound cuts through the static in my head. Sharp. Real.

"Scarletta." His hands stop moving. "Are you OK?"

Am I… OK?

The laugh almost escapes. I feel it burbling inside my chest.

Something dark, and bitter, and completely inappropriate. A sardonic little huff that would say everything my mouth can't form into words.

But then—

He killed him with his bare hands.

He came while doing it.

He could do the same to you.

The laugh dies in my throat. Survival instinct floods through me, cold and clarifying. I know this feeling. I've written this feeling a hundred times—the moment when a character realizes they're in actual danger and their body takes over, does what needs to be done to stay alive.

"Please answer me. I'm worried."

I look at him.

Really look. For the first time since the maze.

His eyes are searching my face, and there's something in them that might be genuine concern. Or maybe just calculation. How big of a threat am I? How damaged? Beyond repair? Does he need to kill me too to keep himself safe?

These questions form and reform on repeat as I nod my head. "Yes," I say. My voice sounds distant. Mechanical. "I'm OK."

His shoulders relax slightly.

"Thank you," I add, because that's what you say, because that's what keeps you safe. "For saving me. He was going to—"

My voice catches.

He was going to do terrible things to you.

And then this man did terrible things to him.

"He hurt me," I finish. "You stopped him."

The unmasked man's hand cups my face. His thumb traces my cheekbone, catching something wet.

Tears. When did I start crying?

"I'll always stop them," he says. "Anyone who tries to hurt you. I'll always stop them."

He leans forward and presses his lips to my forehead. Soft. Careful. Like I'm something fragile that might shatter.

Then my cheeks. One, then the other. Kissing away the tears I can't seem to control.

His mouth finds mine and the kiss is—

Tender.

That's the word. Not hungry. Not demanding. Just gentle pressure, his lips warm against mine, asking nothing.

I cry harder.

He pulls back and resumes washing me. Methodical. Thorough. The cloth moves down my legs, between my toes, back up again. He tips my head back to rinse my hair, supporting my neck with one hand.

None of it is sexual.

All of it is careful.

When he lifts me from the tub, I don't resist. He wraps me in a towel so soft it feels like being swaddled in clouds, patting me dry with the same meticulous attention he gave to washing me.

"Arms up."

I raise them. He slides a white button-down shirt over my head—his shirt, I realize, recognizing the smell of him on the fabric. Then white boxer shorts that pool around my hips until he helps me fold the waistband over. Once. Twice. Three times before they'll stay up.

"Sit."

I sit on the edge of the tub. He produces a comb from somewhere and works it through my wet hair, starting at the ends, patient with the tangles.

No one has combed my hair since I was eight years old.

The tears come again, silent this time.

He doesn't comment. Just keeps combing until my hair lies smooth against my shoulders.

Then he picks me up and carries me outside.

The night air is warm. Stars overhead. The sound of waves somewhere in the distance.

A plane waits on the runway. He carries me up the stairs and through the cabin to a tiny room near the back with a lay-flat chair—the kind you see in first class sections of a commercial plane, but wide enough for two people.

He puts me down, then climbs in beside me and wraps his arms around me from behind, pulling me against his chest.

"Sleep," he says.

I sleep.

I sleep for a very long time because the next thing I know, there's that familiar, unmistakable sensation of falling—the subtle shift in pressure and gravity that signals descent.

My stomach dips slightly, and my ears pop as the plane begins dropping altitude. I don't even remember taking off. Don't remember the engines roaring to life, or the accelera-tion down the runway, or the moment the wheels left the ground.

Just the warm circle of his arms around me and then...
nothing.

Blessed, dreamless nothing.

And now... I'm alone. The warm weight of him is gone
from behind me. The space where his body pressed against
mine feels cool now, empty.

I blink slowly, disoriented, my mind still foggy with sleep.
The hum of the engines has changed pitch, a lower,
descending whine that confirms what my body already
knows—we're going to land.

The plane isn't that big, so when I push myself up on one
elbow and lean over the side of the bed, I can see down the
narrow aisle that runs through the cabin.

His legs are stretched out in a seat near the front of the
plane—dark trousers, expensive leather shoes crossed at the
ankle. The relaxed posture of someone completely at ease. I
think he's talking on the phone, his voice a low murmur I
can't quite make out over the drone of the engines, but I can
see one hand gesturing slightly as he speaks.

The descent is sharper now, more pronounced—my ears
pop again and I have to swallow to clear the pressure. And
then we're touching down, the wheels hitting the runway
with that jarring double-thump that always makes my heart
skip. I struggle to sit up properly, pushing tangled hair out of
my face as I twist to look out the small oval window beside
the bed.

The unmasked man appears at my side, materializing
from the front of the cabin with that silent, purposeful grace
I'm starting to recognize as distinctly *his*.

I look up at him, my brain still sluggish and slow, my
thoughts not quite connecting properly. "Shouldn't you have
your seatbelt on?" my mouth asks without my brain's permission, the question coming out flat and automatic, like I'm
reading lines from a script I don't remember learning.

He smiles down at me, and there's something warm in his

expression that I can't quite process right now, something that feels too genuine for this entire surreal situation. "Did you have a nice rest?"

The plane jerks suddenly, engines screaming in reverse thrust as we decelerate hard down the runway, and I have to brace one hand against the wall to keep from pitching forward. I nod in response to his question because words feel like too much effort.

"Good," he says, and his smile widens, showing teeth, reaching his eyes in a way that makes him look almost boyish despite the expensive suit and the overwhelming presence he carries. "I've got a limo waiting." He jerks his head toward the tarmac outside the window, where I can just make out the sleek black shape of a car gleaming in what looks like late afternoon sunlight. "You'll be home in thirty minutes."

Home. The word echoes strangely in my chest, hollow and foreign. I don't know what home even means anymore. It's been so long since I had a fucking home, the word feels like something ancient. Something lost.

I smile back at the unmasked man anyway, the expression pulling at my face like I'm wearing someone else's skin. Nodding again because it's easier than speaking, easier than trying to untangle the knot of confusion, and exhaustion, and lingering disorientation in my head. "Thanks."

The plane shudders to a complete stop, the whine of the engines dropping to a lower idle, and he reaches down to help me disentangle from the blankets.

His hands are gentle but firm, pulling the soft cashmere away from where it's twisted around my legs, and then he's steadying me, his palm against my lower back as I stand on shaky legs and start walking toward the exit.

My body feels disconnected, like I'm piloting it from a distance—one foot in front of the other, down the narrow aisle past the galley and the seats he'd been occupying earlier.

The door at the front of the cabin is already open, late afternoon light spilling in along with a rush of cool air.

He holds my elbow as we descend the stairs, his grip supportive without being controlling. At the bottom, there's smooth tarmac under my feet, and the black limousine is waiting about twenty feet away.

The unmasked man walks me to it with that same steady hand on my elbow, opens the door, and waits while I duck my head and slide across the buttery leather seat. The windows are tinted so dark, the world outside looks dim and distant.

He settles in beside me, pulling the door shut with a solid, final *thunk* that seals us into the quiet, climate-controlled space.

The silence becomes awkward immediately for some reason. He clears his throat. "So... I... I'm not sure if you've figured it out yet, but... I... like you, Scarletta. I know how this all started was... weird, so it's possible you haven't realized that I like you yet..."

Weird is not the word I would use to describe what 'this' has been.

"But I do," he continues. "And I'm hoping you like me too."

For a moment, neither of us says anything. That awkwardness is thick enough to slice with a knife now.

The scoff I've been holding in finally comes out as I turn to look at him. "I don't even know your *fucking name*."

He laughs a little here. Like I said something funny. "It's Caleb. Caleb MacLeay."

I nod, looking him in the eyes. "OK... Caleb. Well... I'm just—"

"It's all right," he says, hurriedly putting up a hand. "I'm not expecting you to make any kind of commitment right now. You've been through a lot. I just want you to know that I enjoyed our time together and... would like to see you again.

Minus—" he waves one hand through the air, like he's trying to clear something away. "Minus the games, ya know?"

The words hit me sideways, scrambling in my brain before they finally slot into place. When they do, laughter bubbles up from somewhere deep in my chest—sharp, disbelieving, edged with something that might be hysteria. "You want to *date* me?" The question comes out louder than I intended, echoing in the confined space of the car. "Like... dinner and a movie? Coffee shops and holding hands in public?"

He presses his lips together—not quite a smile, not quite a grimace—and nods slowly, deliberately. His eyes never leave mine. "I do. But if you're not ready for that yet, I understand. Take whatever time you need." He pauses, and his voice drops lower, softer. "I'll wait."

I stare at him, my mind spinning uselessly like wheels stuck in mud.

What is this man's deal?

What the *actual fuck* is his fucking deal?

He's been stalking me for months, bought me in a Christmas auction that wasn't even real—just a premise, really—so he could reenact scenes from my book. Which, by the fucking way, ended up with me blacking out and losing memories!

Then he took me to an island under the guise of a Valentine's Day scavenger hunt meant to bolster my trust in him—which worked! I *did* trust him.

I trusted him to keep me safe so explicitly, I put a blindfold on, put ear buds in, and walked into an elaborately staged psychological gauntlet based on a story I wrote in the privacy of my own twisted imagination that ended up being part of some... *seriously* fucking twisted—I don't even know what that was.

I don't understand that man's presence in my maze.

Why was he there?

I'm not going to ask because clearly, he wasn't supposed to

be. He was there to hurt me, that's all I understand. And he did.

He fucking *did.*

And then he got tortured and murdered for it.

And now, Caleb, the masked-unmasked man, is sitting here in a luxury car offering me... what?

A relationship?

Romance?

The kind of normal I've never been able to sustain even when I tried?

And invitation to the St. Patrick's Day... fucking... leprechaun dungeon amusement park?

What? What is he offering me here?

The limo rolls to a stop and I realize that I'm home. Or—whatever this fucking apartment building is.

Caleb smiles, then opens the door and gets out, offering me his hand.

I don't take it. I scramble out, the cold Idaho air hitting me in a real way that it didn't back at the airport, and I walk right past him.

"It's OK," he calls after me. "I'll wait."

I go inside, climbing the steps up to my floor, my hands shaking as I approach my door and realize I don't have my phone, or my key—but when I try the handle, it's open.

Of course, it's open.

This man, this masked, unmasked Caleb man, controls everything.

Everything but the weird old Russian murderer who made his way into my rape-fantasy sex maze, killed my attendants, and...

I slam the door behind me and what do I see on the counter, but my phone and my keys. Plus the clothes I wore to the island—his clothes, I remind myself. Smelling freshly laundered and folded neatly.

I lock the door, crawl into my blanket fort that is now a

glamping tent, and find my laptop still open, waiting for me, but dead because it ran out of battery.

I plug it in to the charger and for a moment I just breathe…

Softly, slowly, in and out.

Then I pick up a glass half full of water on the tiny table next to the laptop, reach up, grab each of the cameras mounted on the inside of the tent, and drop them into the water.

I scramble back out of the tent, get a step ladder from the entryway closet, and one by one, I do this for every camera in my apartment.

Then, I go back to my laptop, turn it on, find the file on my desktop, and disable the keylogging hack.

Fuck. This.

Fuck all of this.

Because what just happened to me wasn't *fun*.

It wasn't a fantasy, it was a fucking *nightmare*.

I am a freak.

I am nothing but a freak.

But fuck it. That's fine. I can live with it. I can live with 'freak'.

What I can't live with is this man.

This unmasked man, this Caleb.

Because he's a goddamned *monster*.

And going back to him… would make *me* one too.

———

Story Fodder #3
Masks don't fool masked men
DEAD DAZE
new york times bestselling author
ja huss

6 Months. No Answers. No Closure. No Contact.

ScarletSins

Check here if you've moved on. I have a new apartment.

Check here if you've forgotten him. I write in coffee shops now.

This is my life. Normal. Safe. Boring. I date men who don't know my real name. I drink lattes and pretend I'm someone who drinks lattes.

Why am I doing this?

Because the alternative is admitting I'm still his.

Six months. No answers. No closure. No contact.

I'm fine.

Watcher

Check here if you've given her space. I follow from three cars back.

Check here if you've stopped watching. I've memorized her new coffee order.

This is my restraint. No cameras. No contact. No crossing the lines she drew. I watch her pretend to write. Pretend to date. Pretend to be someone who forgot me.

Why am I doing this?

Because she asked me to leave her alone.

Then she laughed at his joke.

And I remembered—I never agreed to let her go.

Some monsters know how to wait. Others just learn when to stop.

VIBE WARNINGS

🖤💔🔥 Second Chance Romance
🏃⛓️👁️ She Ran / He Followed
🔥👁️⛓️ Jealous MMC
👁️🔪🖤 Stalker Hero
🪦⛓️💀 He Never Let Go
🔪🖤🔥 Obsessive Hero
👀📚🍌 He Reads Her Books
😈⛓️🖤 She's Mine
💀⚔️🔥 Touch Her and Find Out
🖤🥀💀 Pitch Black MMC
🐺🏃🔥 Predator / Prey
💰⛓️🏙️ Claimed by a Billionaire
🏃💍⛓️ The Chase
👵🔥🖤 Age Gap
🏙️⛓️🖤 Power Imbalance
🚩💀🖤 Did I Mention Pitch Black?

END OF BOOK SHIT

Welcome to the End of Book Shit. This is where I get to say anything I want about the book you just read. It's never edited, excuse my typos, and buckle up, buttercup—this one got interesting…

Because somewhere along the way between a Christmas Sex Auction and a V-Day Hunt in a maze… I started to like these people.

Even though Scarletta is somewhat of a defeatist (am I'm literally the antithesis of a defeatist) I relate to her a little. I get the desire to write like manic, feral idiot. I've been doing it for 13 years now and I have, not once—NOT EVER—run out of shit to write.

It just pours out of me.

I will say that it has been a pretty long time since I wrote erotica. I did quite a bit of it—even if dressed up as Romantic Suspense—earlier in my career. But I drifted pretty far away from erotic over the years. I'd forgotten how fun it was to write.

Times have changed a lot since 2013 though. And the world of spicy dark romance can be a literal landmine. I mean

—for fuck's sake, who hasn't been cancelled at least once at this point, right?

I honestly wish I could get me some of that cancel culture. Lol. Surely I have written things that will enrage the Karens. If I had one hope for 2026 it would be that I'd be cancelled. Massively, global phenomenon cancelled. Let's make this happen!!!

J/K.

I am the only semi-famous person on the earth who does not want to be famous.

But here is what's very different about who I was in 2013 and who I am in 2026.

I have never given any fucks. But everyone says that, don't they. It still bugs them a little when readers get all unhinged about shit. So I did some adjusting back in the day. I will admit that I tried to make my stories 'more acceptable'. More 'mainstream'.

And let's just face it—that's just not what I write.

And 2026 JA Huss gives even fewer fucks about pleasing people now than she did back in the day.

I am going to do my thing.

If people want to come along and see what I've got to say, you are all welcome.

But I'm not going to change my stories for anyone.

If this isn't your book, if you didn't like it, then it wasn't written for you.

But if this was your book, if you DID like it, then it definitely WAS written for you.

And I say that I got interested in these people like it was a surprise.

But I've been invested in all of them.

Every Scarletta who came before her. Every Ashleigh, Every Rook, Every Ivy, every Blue, every Indie, every Wendy, every single fucking Sasha.

I love all these broken black-hearted girls.

There is a place for them in this world, even if that place exists only in the pitch black darkness of my mind.

I would not say I'm very much like Scarletta, though I do see some of her habits in my own daily life.

I write every day. With the exception of my vacation last summer and that one day between every finished book and every new one, I write every day.

I'm not one of those writers who finds it agonizing. I find writing mediative. It's almost a religious experience for me.

So she and I have that in common.

I'm also very much a loner. Mofo's I don't know why, because I've always had friends. I'm not a social person who goes up to people and says hi, but for some reason I attract the butterfly people. They just come to me. And I'm fine with that, but if I go all week and don't even leave my house to check the mail—that's normal.

I remember during Covid I didn't even drive my car for months. It was my truck, actually. That's all I had at the time. And I went so long not driving it, the battery died. Lol

I'm just a loner. So Scarletta and I have that in common.

And while I don't fantasize about the spicy stuff the way she does, nor it is ever the most compelling reason for me to write a story (with the exception of this one, actually) I absolutely do find the whole power exchange thing to be… I don't know… interesting?

Like… why do people like that?

Why is it so compelling?

I haven't studied it, so I'm not sure.

But there definitely IS a pull there.

There's something about giving up control that's both thrilling and horrifying in the same breath.

I'm absolutely y certain that most of you reading this book know more about it than I do. I wonder what your take is on it…

• • •

Anyway. Caleb.

Caleb, my bro, you're just… wow.

There is one more book. I get it, this one had a cliffy. But mo-fo's, the third one is already written. I'm gonna release it the last week of January, so chill man. Chill.

I'm in the process of booking narrators for this audiobook - it won't be released until next fall because this whole thing is 'technically' a Christmas story and I'm not in a hurry to spend $12,000 on a duet narration so I can let it sit on my hard drive for 6 months, because Christmas books don't sell in June.

Plus, I literally have an audiobook coming back from the production company every month from March to August and ouch, the narration bill is adding up.

This one will have to wait.

But good news, it will be one book. One, long 150K book - so that's about 15 hours. Maybe 16, depending on the narrators. It'll be an omnibus and I think you'll love it if you're in to audiobooks.

The third book will be the end of these two - at least for a while. I might revisit them some time in the future. But their journey will wrap up in book 3.

Will they get back together?

I mean… it's romance, so… yes.

But what that looks like, you'll have to wait and see.

Anyway, Happy New Year. It's New Years Day right now as I pen this. I've spent the entire day proofing and this EOBS is the last step. I will upload the book to Amazon tomorrow and that's that.

My first new book of 2026.
Bring it on, let's make this new year RING!

Thank you for reading, thank you for reviewing, and I'll see you in the next book!

Julie
JA Huss
January 1, 2026

ABOUT THE AUTHOR

JA Huss is a scientist, New York Times and USA Today bestselling author. Her self-published romantasy Sparktopia was named an Audible Editors' Best of the Year selection in 2024, and several of her audiobooks have been nominated for the Audie and SOVA Awards. A 2019 RITA finalist, Huss has had five books optioned for film and television and co-wrote a television pilot for MGM with actor and screenwriter Jonathan McClain.